OPERATION FROG EFFECT

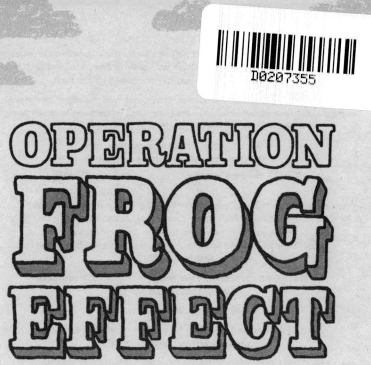

SARAH SCHEERGER

A Yearling Book

Text copyright © 2019 by Sarah Scheerger
Cover art copyright © 2019 by Andy Smith
Interior illustrations copyright © 2019, 2020 by Gina Perry
Emoji copyright © Apple Inc.

All rights reserved. Published in the United States by Yearling, an imprint of Random House Children's Books, a division of Penguin Random House LLC, New York. Originally published in hardcover in the United States by Random House Children's Books, a division of Penguin Random House LLC, New York, in 2019.

Yearling and the jumping horse design are registered trademarks of Penguin Random House LLC.

Visit us on the Web! rhcbooks.com

Educators and librarians, for a variety of teaching tools, visit us at RHTeachersLibrarians.com

The Library of Congress has cataloged the hardcover edition of this work as follows:
Names: Scheerger, Sarah Lynn, author.
Title: Operation frog effect / Sarah Scheerger.
Description: New York: Random House Books for Young Readers, 2019. | Told from eight perspectives, one in graphic novel form, one through poetry, and one as a movie script. | Summary: "Ms. Graham's fifth-grade class wants to promote change in the world; but when eight of them take an assignment too far, they must take responsibility for their actions and unite for a cause they all believe in" —Provided by publisher.
Identifiers: LCCN 2018030807 | ISBN 978-0-525-64412-5 (hardcover) | ISBN 978-0-525-64413-2 (hardcover library binding) | ISBN 978-0-525-64414-9 (ebook)
Subjects: | CYAC: Responsibility—Fiction. | Schools—Fiction. | Teachers—Fiction.
Classification: LCC PZ7.S34244 Ope 2019 | DDC [Fic]—dc23

ISBN 978-0-525-64415-6 (paperback)

Printed in the United States of America
10 9 8 7 6 5 4 3 2 1
First Yearling Edition 2020

Random House Children's Books supports the First Amendment and celebrates the right to read.

Especially for Ben, Noah, Jacob, and Ella.
You make the world a better place.

CHAPTER 1

BLAKE

EMILY

Status: 😄

Dear Hope,

Ms. Graham said we could give our journal a name (so we feel like we're writing to a real person). I've always liked the name Hope. It sounds so optimistic. Okay, I just reread that and *duh!* Of course "hope" sounds optimistic. That's basically the definition, right?

I'm feeling pretty hope*ful* about my First Day of Fifth Grade! We're the kings and queens of White Oak Elementary! I've got both my besties in my class—Aviva (my number one) and Kayley (close second). They came today with matching bracelets (I bet they'll surprise me with one too). They're sitting together in the back of the room. I wish they'd grabbed seats at my table, but oh well. Maybe they didn't see me when they came in?

I can't believe Ms. Graham let us pick our own seats. She looks kinda young, maybe that's why? I hope she winds up being cool. She's gonna lock up the journals at the end of every day. My secrets will be safe with you, Hope, right?

Love and luck,
Emily

PS I think Blake is making frog noises. This doesn't surprise me.

KAYLEY

Dear Ms. Graham,

I *know* you're reading this. I'm tired of pretending I don't know what adults are up to. I'm not being conceited or anything here, Ms. Graham, but I'm harder to fool than other kids.

No offense—but if you *tell* the kids you're not reading the journals, you know half of them won't write at *all*, right? You'll wise up. And then some will be kiss-ups—like Emily, for example. I can see her up front, practically writing a Novel. Aviva and I are outgrowing her. Last year we only sat next to her at lunch to be nice.

Blake Benson is the other one who drives me bananas. Somehow I got stuck with him at my table group, and all he's doing is drawing in his journal and making strange noises under his breath. I hate Blake Benson more than I hate knockoff jeans, and that says a lot. He's basically the cause of every problem.

I'll write every day, like you've asked us to, but I want you to know I'm not fooled. Come on! We're kids! We have Zero Privacy. And anything written at *school* and collected by a *teacher* is most certainly *not private*.

PS I can't even see Blake's mouth moving. Maybe he'll be a ventriloquist someday. That boy needs a plan, because he is *not* good at doing the school thing.

SHARON

I'm going to write my journal in poems.
Sometimes it's easier
To speak the *truth* through a ballpoint pen
Than through my lips.
Probably because no one can interrupt.

When I talk,
I get interrupted (corrected) all the time.
Mostly, people don't want to hear the *truth*.
Instead, they want some softened-up, sugared-over
Version of reality.

Me—I like my truth
Naturally fresh and flavorful
Without added sugar or preservatives.
Just like my food.
We buy organic.

BLAKE ⇒OOPS!⇐

HENRY

Someday I'll be a *real* movie writer/director, and I'll be so famous and rich that I'll pay someone to do the boring things like making my bed and setting the table.

My movies will be comedies. None of that sappy tearjerker junk for me. I think I'm pretty funny. Ma agrees. Not that I'm actually funny, but that I *think* I'm funny. She's always saying, "You think you're so funny."

And I say, "True dat," like a gangsta from a TV show, which makes her frown.

If I'm gonna be rich and famous, I've got to prepare. That's why Ba gave me his old cell phone. It's ancient but it has service (sometimes) and takes videos and photos, so I can practice making movies. I'll practice in my journal too, by writing scenes instead of regular boring journal entries. Ms. Graham said we could write our journals any way we want, so here goes. The dollar signs ($) below are for inspiration.

$$

SCENE: *5th-grade classroom at White Oak Elementary School, 32 students sitting at desks in groups of 4. Ms. Graham moves her hands when she talks, like she's conducting an invisible orchestra.*

MS. GRAHAM: Look around you. The seats you've chosen today will be yours for the whole year.

HENRY: *(whispers to seat partner)* Rats! Should've sat closest to the door.

EMILY: *(raises hand)*

MS. GRAHAM: *(conducts)* Get to know your table groups because you'll need to work cooperatively for each assignment. We'll be learning through hands-on group projects. Yes . . . Emily?

EMILY: Since we didn't know about yearlong table groups when we sat down, can we switch today before we get started?

MS. GRAHAM: Great question! And thank you for warming us up by being the first to raise your hand. But no . . . the table groups are set. I do this on purpose so that students have a chance to work through any peer problems that arise.

KAYLEY: *(raises hand)* Will we be graded individually or as a team?

MS. GRAHAM: As a team.

KAYLEY: *(looks at our table group and sighs)*

HENRY: *(under breath to Kayley)* Okay, this is how it'll be. You work, and I'll supervise. *(Henry spies a frog leaping from Blake's pocket. It hops away from the table.)*

KAYLEY: Eek! *(scrambles onto her chair and points)* Ms. Graham! THERE'S A FROG BY YOUR FOOT!

MS. GRAHAM: Well, hello there. *(surprisingly calm, picks up frog)* He's injured.

KAYLEY: *(shrieking)* Now there's a FROG IN YOUR HAND!!!!!

MS. GRAHAM: So there is. *(smiles)* First class vote of the year: What do you all propose we do with this frog?

KAI

Dear Frog,

Yes, I'm writing to you.

At this moment, you're the single most interesting thing in this class.

Wait—is Emily crying? She keeps sniffling and poking her fingers at the corners of her eyes. She usually hooks up with Kayley and Aviva for projects. But this time she's got me,

Sharon, and that new girl Cecilia (who started at White Oak last year). Cecilia smells like flowery girl shampoo.

Maybe Emily's sorry she's stuck with us. I kind of want to reassure her that I'll be a good team member. Just because I finish my work super-fast and teachers are always after me for reading under my desk, that doesn't mean I'm a slacker. Classwork is so easy that I can finish it all, get 100%, and still read half a novel during the school day. That's not being a slacker, that's being efficient. Same philosophy at home. I can read and mop at the same time. Don't bother asking me how (I refuse to reveal my secret method).

We're a big reading family. Maybe because both my parents are education professors at the university. They stagger their teaching schedules so that someone's always home for the four of us kids after school, and we all pitch in to help. Everyone in my house has got lots to say . . . all the time. Sometimes the only way to get away from them is to hide in the coat closet with a flashlight and read.

Reading is a good thing, right? But guess what I get in the most trouble for? *Reading.* Somehow no one thinks it's a good idea to read while walking the dog, taking out the trash, or mowing the lawn. Apparently, I got all the creative genes.

PS Writing in private journals on shared desks is a recipe for disaster. People will peek. Not me, of course. Other people.

CECILIA

Hola Abuelita,

It's the first day of school, and my teacher held a frog in her bare hands! ¡Guau! I thought that girl Kayley was going to have a heart attack.

We have an assignment to write every day in journals. I'll write to YOU, Abuelita. What better way to practice your English than to read my letters, right? I'll write in English, but I'll translate any words I don't think you'll know. When my journal is full, I'll mail it to you, and you'll know I'm missing you.

Mami misses you too. Mexico is too far. Every night we dream of bringing you back here to stay with us. I remember being a little girl and snuggling up on Mami's lap while you two talked and drank café de olla. "Hungry, mija?" Mami would ask, and I'd shake my head (even though I was starving) because it was so cozy sitting with you both that I didn't want her to move. Hopefully, someday we'll live together again.

Between my letters, our phone calls, that English class you're taking, and watching television from the US—you're gonna be practically fluent! ¡Practica tu inglés!

WORDS TO PRACTICE (I know you can do it!)

journal = *el diario*	heart attack = *el infarto*
assignment = *la tarea*	practice = *práctica*

Besos y abrazos,
Cecilia

AVIVA

Date: September 5

Everyone is *super-excited* about the idea of having a class frog. Ms. Graham let a few students take a break from journaling and convert a big plastic storage container into a frog habitat. They're gathering grass and poking holes in the lid. I'm an amphibian lover, so normally I'd be volunteering to help, but I can't shake a worry.

So here's what happened. Kayley decided we should wear our matching rainbow best-friends bracelets today, and she saved me a place in class this morning. I tried to get Emily's attention and wave her over, but Henry snagged the desk right in front of me, and Blake Benson slid into the seat in front of Kayley. She hates-hates-hates Blake Benson, so I was sure she'd say she was saving that seat. But she didn't.

I elbowed Kayley and whispered, "What about Emily?" But she shrugged and said we had to stop babying Emily all the time.

I real quick scribbled Emily a note, telling her not to stress, that Blake would be moved up front within a week. I've been in Blake's class every year since second grade, and teachers figure him out pretty fast. But then Ms. Graham said we'd be keeping the same seats and the same teams all year. (!!!!) So now I'm sitting here journaling and worrying about whether Emily is upset.

I like writing. Because I'm quiet, people think I don't have much to say, but the opposite is true. I have SO much to say.

I probably have as much to say as Sharon, and she's waving her hand to make a comment every five seconds. Kayley always sighs superduper loud when Sharon's talking. I don't mind Sharon talking so much. She's not my friend or anything, but she makes me think.

CHAPTER 2

VOTING ON A NAME FOR OUR CLASS FROG

NAME IDEAS	# OF VOTES
Kermit	5
Harold	4
Petunia	5
Frog-Gee	4
Mr. Frog	5
Mrs. Frog-arina	4
Ranita (Spanish word for "little frog")	4
Jeremiah (the bullfrog)	1

KERMIT vs. PETUNIA vs. MR. FROG

NAME IDEAS	# OF VOTES
Kermit	12
Mr. Frog	10
Petunia	10

Introducing . . . Kermit!

EMILY

Status: 😶

Dear Hope,

I told Aviva and Kayley that we should all write Ms. Graham letters to ask her to let us be in the same group. I was way too scared to go straight up to Ms. Graham and talk to her about it. Especially after she shut me down in class. But I thought maybe if Aviva and Kayley and I all wrote her . . . she'd listen?

Aviva smiled and nodded at first, but then after Kayley said, "Can't you take a hint? She already told you no," Aviva stopped nodding.

Well, I'm going to write one anyway. Kayley and Aviva are acting strange. I'm not sure what's up? They've been wearing their rainbow bracelets all week (but never gave me one). And I just noticed they had matching ankle bracelets today too.

Love and luck,
Emily

———

Dear Ms. Graham,

I know you said "no changing groups." I promise I'm not trying to argue. I want you to know that Aviva, Kayley, and I have been best friends since second grade. Mom says it's hard to have a group of three, because someone can be left out. But it's not normally like that for us.

Only now they're laughing at jokes I don't understand, and

dressing like twins, and eating their lunches really fast before I even sit down.

This is our last year together. Kayley's parents are putting her in a private middle school. So she'll be leaving the rest of us. That's why this year is extra important.

This will all be better if you put me in their group. Please?

From Emily

AVIVA

Date: September 8

Kayley says we have to let Emily make new friends, that it's for her own good. This hurts my heart, but she's probably right. Emily *only* hangs out with us, and we *only* hang out with her, so it usually works out okay.

But I just found out that Ima and Aba (that's what I call my parents) are sending me to La Ventana Prep next year for middle school. *Say what?* I thought I'd stay in public school. Kayley's going to La Ventana too. Her parents reserved a spot there when she was in kindergarten. My parents signed me up last week (*before* they talked to me about it, by the way).

Ima and Aba said they'd heard horror stories about public middle school. *Horror stories?* What exactly does that mean? When I asked, all I got was *bullies-and-cigarettes*. So middle school has bullies? Big whoop. Bullies are everywhere. I'll survive. And do my parents seriously think I'd try a cigarette?

I may not be a genius, but I'm not a complete idiot either. I like my teeth white and my lungs pink, thank you very much.

No matter how much I argued that I'd be fine in public middle school, they couldn't hear me. I told them that La Ventana is all girls and probably all rich girls. I won't fit in at all. But then they said it's the only non-Christian-based private school in the county (we're Jewish), and public middle school is not-on-the-table, so it's La Ventana or back to homeschooling. Yikes. They hugged me and told me they just want what's best for me. They are *so* strict, and they think they know best *all the time*.

This is *exactly* why I don't share my thoughts. It's like I'm yelling underwater and all I'm getting is wet. After a while I stopped arguing and sat there, deflated like a balloon.

PS I'm worried about the frog. I did some research last night and found out that wild frogs have difficulty surviving in captivity. The trick is to make sure you know the type of species, so you can have the right habitat. I printed out the article, but I don't want Ms. Graham to think I'm trying to tell her what to do. Maybe I'll just set the article on her desk at recess.

SHARON

I work *alone*.
Mostly.
Sure, I sit in a table group.

Sure, we talk.
But they all think I'm weird.

It's okay.
I *am* weird.
I don't have three eyes
Or purple polka dots,
But there's something about me
That's different.
And sometimes,
Different means strange.

Mom says it's because I don't care
About what other people think.
But she's wrong.
I *do* care about what people think.
I find it fascinating.
But I don't care to change ME in order to make them like me.

KAYLEY

Dear Ms. Graham,

   Emily's going to write you a letter, asking you to switch her group. No offense to Emily, but we don't *want* to be in her group.

   Emily will need to find new friends before middle school, since Aviva and I are both going to La Ventana Prep next year.

She's way too dependent on us. If we keep hanging out with her, she'll never branch out. It's for her own good.

There's no way Emily's mom could afford to send her to La Ventana. Emily's smart enough—but they only give full scholarships to geniuses. Poor Emily—her dad took off to explore faraway places like Lebanon and Armenia, and her mom paints for a living (for real) and practically makes no money. Sucks to be Emily.

PS No offense, Ms. Graham. But it's kind of a waste of time for us to be researching types of frogs. A frog is a frog is a frog! Who cares what kind it is? It's gross no matter what!

EMILY

Status: 😢
Dear Hope,

Ms. Graham called me up to her desk to talk today. I got that "oh no I'm in trouble" feeling. My throat tightened up right away. I couldn't meet her eyes, so I stared at her dangly earrings.

She thanked me for my letter but said it was important to keep the seats consistent. Right away I felt tears pushing at the bridge of my nose. I hadn't cried in school since third grade, and I sure didn't want to break my record. Ms. Graham started to say something else, but I just needed to get out of there because those tears were about to burst free.

After lunch, I found this note on my desk.

Dear Emily,

We spoke briefly today, but I wanted to add a few thoughts. Please know that I admire it when students stand up for themselves. I understand your reasons for wanting to switch groups. However, let's give our seating arrangement a chance. If you're still concerned about this issue in a few months, we can always take it to a class vote. Let's wait until after Thanksgiving and see how you feel then.

In life, the most challenging experiences are also the most rewarding. I encourage you to stick it out. Spread your wings and try something different. This is how we grow.

I want to tell you that your letter sparked an idea. Mailboxes! We'll all make mailboxes for our desks, myself included, and send each other letters throughout this year.

Thanks for helping *me* "think outside the box."

Sincerely,

Ms. Graham

PS Talk to Sharon. She has lots to say.

I wanted to rip her letter into shreds. Doesn't she know she's RUINING my life?

—Emily

HENRY

SCENE: *Students mill about the room and work on a babyish project—making mailboxes out of wrapping-paper-covered shoe boxes.*

KAI: Can I swap with someone? The only wrapping paper we had at home has floating babies and rattles.

HENRY: I have silver. You want silver?

KAI: Thank you. You saved my life.

HENRY: My powers surprise even me.

AVIVA: Did you see that Ms. Graham is wrapping her box in froggie-covered wrapping paper? I wonder if she had that at home or if she bought it just for this.

KAYLEY: Who cares? Wrapping paper and letter writing are both killing trees. It's entirely ungreen and global-warming-ish.

HENRY: That's not a word.

KAYLEY: You knew what I meant.

BLAKE: This is a trick to make us write more.

HENRY: *(all theatrical)* Curses! The scoundrel's trying to force us to learn! I'm onto her sneaky plan!

AVIVA: *(softly)* It *is* kinda fun, though. It might be fun to write letters too.

HENRY: No way! You sounded like Minnie Mouse just then.

AVIVA: *(turns red)*

HENRY: Maybe you should do voice-over work in cartoons. I have an auntie who does that. She's got a high-pitched voice too.

AVIVA: Uh. O-kay.

KAYLEY: Is everything a joke to you?

HENRY: Yep. Pretty much. Haven't we been over this before? It's called wit.

KAYLEY: Yeah, maybe *dim*wit.

BLAKE: *I* think you're funny.

HENRY: See? Someone who appreciates my humor.

CECILIA

Hola Abuelita,

Today I put stickers all over my journal and added some to my mailbox. I don't want anyone to mistake my journal for theirs. I'm sharing my heart with you, Abuelita, but I don't want anyone from my class reading my private thoughts. Ms. Graham promises she's not reading our journals either. Don't worry, I remember what you said—I know to be careful about sharing our situation.

Ms. Graham is funny. She puts all these sticky notes around her desk to remind her to do things. Some of them are practical, like "Pick up dog food after work" or "Prep for Tuesday's lesson." Those practical sticky notes disappear (and then new ones appear) each day. But she also has silly sticky notes that just stay stuck day after day. Like "Breathe" or "Be. Here. Now." or "Being in the now." What do you think, Abuelita? If she can't remember to breathe, she might have a bigger problem than a hungry dog.

If I wrote myself a silly reminder sticky note like Ms. Graham's, it would be "Relax." No one needs to remind me to breathe. I've got that one down.

Guess what? I'm starting to like Kermit! Remember how I used to get all creeped out by lizards? Kermit's a whole different story. I stop by his habitat/tank every morning and say, "Hola ranita." I swear he stares right at me and says, "Croá, croá." Looks like I've got a new friend, Abuelita.

WORDS TO PRACTICE
stickers = *calcomanías*

Besos y abrazos,
Cecilia

BLAKE WASTING CLASS TIME 101

SHARON

I slipped a note
In Blake Benson's mailbox.
All it said was
"Have a Nice Day!"
Because he doesn't fit in either.
He tries to, but it's like he's mixed up
Being cool with being bad
And thinks one equals the other.

Blake feeds the frog fresh
Crunchy crickets and
Hangs out by the habitat.
Maybe he's watching, worried
Kermit won't recover from HER* injuries.
Or maybe it's just another way Blake
Can avoid the mean kids.

He cares that he doesn't fit,
I see it in the way
His shoulders hunch and his mouth curves down.
He notices the way
The others scramble and scooch
To the middle of the lunch benches
So that there is no room for him.

*(Why does everyone assume that the frog is a boy?)

I invite him over to my table in the corner,
But it doesn't make his shoulders straighten out.
It's easier to be like me . . .
And not care.

CHAPTER 3

FUN FROG FACTS: TABLE GROUP ACTIVITY

Research and gather as many Fun Frog Facts as you can.

As soon as you find one, write it on a sticky note.

Complete as many sticky notes as possible.

You have thirty minutes.

And . . . go!

(Candy frog gummies will be involved. No actual frogs were injured in the making of these gummies.)

Frogs shed their skin once a week, then EAT it!
YUCK!
Frogs drink water through their skin instead of through their mouths.
Most frogs have teeth in their upper jaw.
Hi!
Male Darwin frogs swallow developing tadpoles. They keep them in their vocal sacs until they are ready to come out as juvenile frogs.
LOL
A group of frogs is called an army.
Eww!
Male frogs attract female frogs by croaking (not the dying kind of croaking but the sound kind of croaking).
MANY FROGS CAN LEAP MORE THAN 20 TIMES THEIR BODY LENGTH.
!!!
The golden poison dart frog has enough venom to kill ten grown men.

AVIVA

Date: September 12

Every time I see Emily, my stomach hurts.

This morning she put a note in my mailbox.

> Aviva,
>> What's going on?
>> Please talk to me. Maybe we can walk to school
> together tomorrow?
>>> Your bestie since second grade,
>>> Emily

That last line made my throat prickle. Emily and I have been best friends ever since I rescued her. Two weeks after Ima stopped homeschooling me, she enrolled me in second grade. All the kids knew each other already, and everyone had paired up. Emily and I were seat buddies, but I don't think we said more than ten words to each other until I lied for her.

Cranky Ms. McFarley never let us use the bathroom after recess. This was supposed to teach us to use-our-time-wisely and be-responsible-enough to go potty instead of play handball all recess long. Really this taught us to hold our pee longer.

One time Emily couldn't hold it . . . and she wound up peeing a big old puddle in her chair. I told everyone I'd spilled my water bottle and she'd sat in it. When Emily came back to class with fresh loaner shorts from the nurse's office, she shot me this grateful look, and we became instant best friends. Suddenly school was fantasterrific.

We got even closer when her parents divorced, because Emily wanted to sleep over a lot. My parents prefer to host the sleepovers, because "overprotective" is their middle name, so having Emily over was a win-win.

Kayley's our third—even though she and Emily hung out before I came along. Kayley's the kind of friend you have to be careful not to make mad. Sometimes she can be mean.

Only now, *everything* is changing and I don't know how to stop it. I need to stay on Kayley's good side because we'll be together next year. I don't want to have to sit alone at lunch. The chance that I'll rescue another friend from a puddle of pee . . . is low.

I can't walk with Emily because Kayley will get mad and Emily will ask me questions I don't know how to answer. I can just imagine her saying, "You know how Kayley is. Why're you letting her make all the decisions? Don't you have your own opinion?" And I'd be all . . . "(silence)." Because what can I say to that? Of *course* I have opinions. I have tons of them. But *having* them doesn't mean I can *share* them, or stand up to Kayley about them.

I slipped a note in Emily's box right before lunch.

Dear Emily,
I'm getting a ride tomorrow. We'll talk soon.
Aviva

Truth—I'm *not* getting a ride tomorrow, but I can walk a different way to school. That way I won't run into Emily. Sometimes life is so complicated.

BLAKE

KAYLEY

Dear Ms. Graham,

Not to be a Tattletale, but do you know that Blake is only drawing in his journal? Every day? How does he get away with that? Don't you notice when you walk around? Just because he goes to Resource Class for English doesn't mean you should let him slack off.

And can you please give Sharon a quota for comments? That girl needs to zip it! Teachers always think she's brilliant, but the truth is that she reads history books for fun. *Who does that?*

No offense, but has anyone explained to you the purpose of sticky notes? They're to *remind* you do to things. You've got at least twelve on your desk right now. That's like reminder overload. I'm not sure it's helpful. And do you really need a note to remind you to "Laugh Often"? *Puh-leeze.*

Last thing: Don't you think it's unsanitary to have students bringing in bugs for Kermit to eat? I know you've got that antibacterial hand wash, but still. *Gross.*

PS I will tell Emily that Aviva's going to La Ventana soon. *Awkward.*

CHAPTER 4

> **MY CLASS = YOUR CLASS = OUR CLASS**
>
> Select your class job this week.
>
> Choose wisely—it's yours for the year.

HENRY

SCENE: *Table group work. Students discuss class job options, including the class council election coming up on Friday. Happy, wasting-class-time buzz fills the room.*

HENRY: I'm voting for Kermit. He'll bring class council to a whole new level.

KAYLEY: You bring "annoying" to a whole new level.

HENRY: What? Kermit is the perfect candidate—he's calm, he won't gossip, he can jump more than twice his body length. All good qualities for a leader.

MS. GRAHAM: Remember, this Friday's vote is not a popularity contest.

KAYLEY: *(whispers)* It's TOTALLY a popularity contest. That's why I'm not running. I might get it and I don't want it.

HENRY: Seriously—you SHOULD run. You could abolish homework.

KAYLEY: *(makes a face)*

HENRY: Or expand our snack choices.

KAYLEY: Why don't YOU run, if you've got so many ideas?

HENRY: I'm a behind-the-scenes kind of guy. I'll write your acceptance speech.

KAYLEY: Shut up! I can't tell when you're being serious and when you're just kidding.

HENRY: That's because you're not familiar with Henryish.

KAYLEY: What is Henryish?

HENRY: My language. You know, like English or Spanish. . . . I speak Henryish.

KAYLEY: You are so strange.

HENRY: Thank you. I take that as a compliment.

KAYLEY: *(sighs)*

EMILY

Status: 🙄
Dear Hope,

Truthfully, I want to boycott this whole class job assignment. (I'm still MAD at Ms. Graham for not letting me change my table group.) But if I HAVE to pick SOMETHING, I'm going to run for class council. If some of the kids are going to be making our classroom rules, I want to be a part of it.

The problem is that I don't have a ton of friends, but I'll need a TON of votes. I've always hung out with Aviva and Kayley, only they've been acting so weird recently. Today I'm going to try to talk to three new people at lunch. I've known most of these kids since kindergarten (and I think they'll vote for me), but who knows? Now I'm wishing I'd had bigger birthday parties. Birthday parties buy friends.

I wish I could talk to my parents about some of these things. But Dad's traveling, like always. Sometimes I HATE my dad's job. Him being gone (practically ALL the time) is the main reason my parents got a divorce. I used to talk to Mom about drama at school, but she always says she's not feeling 100%, so these days I just don't want to worry her.

> Still feeling unlucky and hope*less*,
> Emily

PS Sometimes I think I might want to be a journalist when I grow up, but if I do, I'll do it better than Dad. I'll make time for my family.

AVIVA

Date: September 13

My hand is shaking so badly that I can hardly write. The *scariest* thing just happened!!!

I walked the long way to school this morning. I didn't want to run into Emily, especially since I'd told her I had a ride. All of a sudden, a banged-up car pulled up next to me real slow. This scruffy man sat inside. He had tattoos up and down his arms. He'd crammed his car so full of clothes, food, laundry detergent, and trash that I doubted he could see out the windows. I felt like I'd stepped into one of those "Stranger Danger" ads, because just like all the stories, Tattoo Man rolled down the window and asked, "Have you seen my dog? He ran off. He's a long-haired black Lab."

I told him "no" and "sorry," then kept walking. Only just then he jerked the wheel, parked at the curb, and got out of the car! I panicked. Probably he was just climbing out to look for his dog, but it *totally* freaked me out! I ran so fast that my chest hurt, and when I turned to look behind me, Tattoo Man was gone.

I bumped into Emily right when I got to school, and I wanted to tell her what happened, but then I'd have to explain why I was walking. I couldn't tell Kayley either because she'd say I'm such-a-baby for getting scared. So I didn't tell anyone. Just sat down and started writing.

At least my journal can't laugh at me or make me feel stupid.

CECILIA

Hola Abuelita,

I can't imagine running for class council. I'd be way too nervous to give a speech in front of everyone.

Abuelita, remember how I came home from kindergarten and couldn't stop crying because I couldn't understand anyone at school? Of course, now I speak English just as well as anyone, and I can translate for Mami at parent-teacher conferences, but I think that's when I started feeling self-conscious about talking. I'm not shy, I'm just quiet. There's a difference.

At White Oak, the only time I feel totally comfortable is during lunch recess. A bunch of us have soccer matches on the far field. I've been playing goalie—I don't mind diving for the ball, even if the ground is muddy. I'd like to try another position soon. I love soccer, partly because I'm good at it, partly because of all the memories I have of watching fútbol on the couch with you and Abuelito, and partly because the game's the same whether I speak Spanish or English. (I miss Abuelito so much. I know you do too.)

Ms. Graham is asking us to write letters for our class mailboxes every week. Today I made myself write two. Sometimes writing is easier than talking.

WORDS TO PRACTICE
shy = *tímida*

Besos y abrazos,
Cecilia

Dear Ms. Graham,

Every day I see a new frog figure or frog poster in class. You must really like frogs. I think you should add a sticky note that says, "Ribbit!"

From Cecilia

———

Dear Aviva,

What's wrong? You look sad today. If you ever want to talk, let me know.

From Cecilia

HENRY

SCENE: *Students vote for class council. Overachievers stupid enough to run: Amaya, Emily, Kai, and Amar. They're looking nervous and turning shades of green. Ten points if someone barfs.*

MS. GRAHAM: Just a refresher, kids. Our class will be set up kind of like the branches of the US government. We'll elect two council members to represent Congress, while our class judge will represent the courts. And I will represent the president. Here we go *(unfolds a piece of paper)*. . . . Our class council members will be . . . drum roll, please . . . Emily and Kai!

CLASS: *(Some clap, some groan.)*

MS. GRAHAM: And I'm appointing our class judge. This will be . . . Sharon!

CLASS: *(reacts)*

SHARON: *(sinks lower in her seat)*

HENRY: Better luck next time, Kermit. I was rooting for you!

MS. GRAHAM: This is not an exact replica of the government—but it should give you a sense of what it's like to balance different interests and powers for the good of the people. I, of course, will retain veto power, like the president.

BLAKE: *(under breath)* Big surprise.

MS. GRAHAM: In the real United States government, Congress can override a president's veto with a two-thirds vote, but I do have to retain some control over this classroom, so my veto will be final.

KAYLEY: *(whispers)* Basically, she's acting like we've got control, but really we have none.

MS. GRAHAM: I'd also like to remind you that any member of this class can propose a new law.

HENRY: *(whispers back)* I dare you to propose a law. Something outrageous. Like we get to grade ourselves.

KAYLEY: *(sighs and ignores him)*

HENRY: Or double recess, or no homework, or movie Fridays.

BLAKE: I'll do it.

HENRY: Yeah!

MS. GRAHAM: Anyone brave enough to go first?

BLAKE: I want to get rid of homework. We shouldn't have to do work outside of school.

MS. GRAHAM: *(laughs)* I can't blame you for trying. Okay, okay. I'll send your class council out to begin to discuss your proposal.

HENRY: *(fist-bumps Blake)* Thanks, bro. You rock!

BLAKE: *(looks proud)*

KAYLEY: *(rolls eyes)* What a waste of time. You know she's gonna veto it.

HENRY: Kayley. You're missing the point. Wasting class time is a GOOD thing. Get with the program!

KAYLEY: *(sighs)* I'm actually looking forward to an all-girls private school. And they have to wear plaid skirts every single day. That's how irritating you are.

HENRY: Success!

EMILY

Dear Hope,

I can't believe I made it onto class council! Kai and I sat outside at the round lunch tables to discuss Blake's proposal. We both agreed this was pointless. There's no way Ms. Graham would approve getting rid of homework.

Kai showed me how he can solve a Rubik's Cube behind his back. So it wasn't entirely a waste of time. The funny thing was that we did start to talk about Blake's proposal a little. We figured we had to approve this law or we might as well drop out of school, because everyone would hate us. So we were basically passing a law knowing that Ms. Graham would veto it.

And then inspiration struck. What if we proposed only doing half the homework? Like half the math problems? Or half the vocab definitions? Ms. Graham might actually approve that.

So we tried it.

> Love and crossing-my-fingers luck,
> Emily

BLAKE

KAi

Hey, Frog!

Yes!!! Ms. Graham approved our half-homework law! She'll watch our test scores on Fridays, and if our scores go down, she'll veto the law. But if they stay the same, she'll let the law stand. Today at lunch three different guys offered me their chips to thank me. *Sweet!*

After lunch, Ms. Graham set a stack of books on my desk. I guess she's noticed how worn out my favorites are. (I read them over and over until they actually fall apart.)

"Looks like I won't have to convince you to read," she said, smiling, and patted the top of the stack. "Want to branch out and try something new?" I took a quick peek—four new books, all fantasy. *Yes!*

Ms. Graham is the first teacher who hasn't banned me from keeping books in my desk (although it is only the first month of school, so she still has time). I can listen to the teacher and read at the same time, but nobody seems to appreciate this talent.

KAYLEY

Dear Ms. Graham,

My mother's having a Reaction. She's got hives all over, she's so upset. She has a Reaction a couple of times a year. When I was little it freaked me out, but now I bring her cream for her hives, and a diet ginger ale from the garage fridge, and I hide in my room.

My mother thinks it's ridiculous that you're letting the kids run the classroom!!!! Sharon doesn't even know how to pick clothes that match. How can she make important decisions as our judge? Plus my mother can't believe you're letting us do half the homework. She's making *me* do it *all*, by the way. Usually after she has a Reaction, she goes on a Mission to fix the Problem.

In this case, she'd say the Problem is *you*. Be careful, Ms. Graham.

PS I count seven frog-related decorations in the classroom. Eight if you include Kermit. Don't you think that's a bit overboard?

CECILIA

Hola Abuelita,

Last night, I woke up to Mami crying. She saves her tears for after I'm asleep. I couldn't stand to hear her sadness and do nothing. Finally, I got up and made her a cup of té de manzanilla just like she does for me.

Do you know, Abuelita, that she worries about you being all alone without Abuelito to keep you company? I never hear her tell you this during phone calls. I also never hear her share how terrible she feels that she missed a chance to say goodbye to Abuelito in person. It doesn't matter that you told her not to come, that it was too risky, that if she left the US, she might not be able to come back.

Sometimes I wish you didn't take Abuelito back to Mexico. I understand why you did it, because you didn't have medical insurance here, and he was so sick. But I was just seven back then, and I didn't understand that my goodbye to him was final. I don't think Mami understood either.

I know the schools are good in the United States, and I know it's safe here. It's just—I don't want to grow up without you. Someday I'll be old enough to travel to Mexico by myself. But it's so hard to wait.

Maybe I'll buy some sticky notes for the fridge and write Mami a special note—"una sonrisa es algo hermoso." A smile is a beautiful thing.

WORDS TO PRACTICE
travel = *viajar*

> Besos y abrazos,
> Cecilia

Dear Emily,

You rule! I'm so glad you're on class council. Half the homework is a great start. Maybe next . . . longer recesses? Then we might actually be able to finish a soccer game.

> Your friend,
> Cecilia

EMILY

Status: 😦

Dear Hope,

I'm writing you from my bedroom closet. Ms. Graham said we can bring our journals home whenever.

MY LIFE IS OVER!!!!! (I know that sounds overly dramatic, but it's true!) At recess Kayley pranced over to me, acting all important. And Aviva stood there looking at the sky. Then Kayley dropped this colossal bomb. They're BOTH going to La Ventana next year!

WHAT?!!!! I will have NO friends!

None! What will I do? Who will I sit with at lunch?

Unloved and unlucky,
Emily

PS In the old days, before the divorce, I'd have gone downstairs to talk to Mom about this. She'd have brought me a soft blanket and told me some story that had nothing to do with anything but was still nice to hear. I'm not sure why I stopped talking to Mom about sad stuff? Maybe because she doesn't need me adding any more tears to the mix. But crying alone is the WORST.

CHAPTER 5

Dear esteemed students,

Today we'll begin brainstorming for our Egg Drop Challenge. You'll all work cooperatively as table groups to devise a way to protect your eggs. Be scientists and engineers!

GUIDELINES FOR THE EGG DROP CHALLENGE:

- Package your egg with any materials you'd like.
- Egg goes in box (along with whatever else).
- Egg must be raw.
- Ms. Graham will drop egg container off roof.
- Whichever eggs are unbroken after the fall WIN!

Failure to follow these guidelines means immediate disqualification.

SHARON

No matter how smart we all think we are,
And no matter how hard we try

To cushion our eggs,
Some of them are gonna crack.

I know I said I didn't care
What other kids think.
But that's not completely true.
There's a teeny-tiny part of me
That cares a whole lot.
Do you know how many letters I've written to other kids?
Seven.
Do you know how many letters I've gotten in my mailbox?
That'd be a big fat ZERO.
Why?

If I was an egg,
There'd be hairline cracks
Along my sides.
Every time I get hurt feelings,
Another crack zigzags
Across my smooth, hard shell.

KAi

Hey, Frog!

Yesterday I brought my journal home. I wanted to work out some measurements for our egg drop. Only, when I opened it, I realized I'd grabbed the wrong book. I had Blake's instead.

I swear I didn't look.

Well, I didn't look on purpose. I flipped through it, and it took a few seconds to figure out I had the wrong one. (We both have the same exact marbled cover.) By then I'd seen a couple of pages. I didn't realize what a great artist he is.

When I brought it back this morning, all of a sudden I started stressing. Maybe I'd get in trouble for taking his journal. So I was real careful about how I dropped it back in the lockbox. I slid it under my shirt and walked over there on my way to get a drink of water. I dropped it in quick. Nobody saw.

Side note—the key to the Egg Drop Challenge is suspension. In order for the egg not to break, it can't feel the impact. The other teams are all trying to cushion the egg. But I've got a strategy to string the egg into the center of the box, suspended. I'll use a pair of my mom's nylon stockings and put the egg inside. I'll twist and tie the ends so that it stays secure, and then suspend it in the box. When the box hits the ground, the nylon will rebound up and down, but not enough for it to bang into the bottom of the box. The egg won't be jolted, it'll just be a gentle impact. It's my theory, anyway.

I'm usually not a big supporter of class projects (boring), but I'm totally getting into this one. I even spent time last night working on this at home.

PS Now Ms. Graham's giving me a stack of new books every week. (Not all fantasy, though—she's sneaking in realistic fiction too.) Today I'm reading *The Crossover*—and it's the kind of book I want to read out loud, because it's filled up with poetry that sounds like music.

BLAKE

HENRY

SCENE: *Henry circles the room, recording with his phone camera. Ms. Graham grades a mountain of papers.*

TEAM A: Foam packing peanuts?

HENRY: *(from behind camera, whispers to self)* Good idea.

TEAM B: What if we suspend it? With nylon or something?

HENRY: Ooh. Better idea.

AVIVA: *(quietly)* Are you recording them?

HENRY: No. I'm holding this camera up beside my body all sly because I'm NOT recording them.

AVIVA: Turn it off. We could get in trouble.

HENRY: This is purely for research. There's no rule against researching.

KAYLEY: *(hisses)* Shut up, Aviva! You're such a baby. I told him to do that. We need to know what we're up against.

AVIVA: *(quiet)*

KAYLEY: *(walks away)*

AVIVA: I was thinking we could use hay.

HENRY: *(puts camera down)* Good idea. That might work! I'll turn the camera off if it makes you feel weird. I was just joking around.

AVIVA: Thanks. We can come up with our own idea. We don't need anyone else's.

HENRY: True. I forgot we have a genius on our team.

AVIVA: Who? You?

HENRY: Nope. You.

AVIVA: Shut up. *(smiling a little)*

HENRY: I wasn't joking. You're smart. Hey, I didn't mean to hurt your feelings when I said you sound like Minnie Mouse.

AVIVA: That's okay.

HENRY: Sometimes my mouth gets ahead of my brain.

AVIVA: *(looks at Kayley)* You're not the only one.

HENRY: True dat.

SHARON

This assignment
Has put Eggs on my Brain.

If I was an egg myself, I'd be
Soft-boiled—
My firm outsides

Protecting my soft insides
Of gooey, gloppy yolk.

Aviva would be sunny-side up—
Nice to look at,
But easy to puncture.

And Kayley . . . she'd be rotten.
Slimy, stinky, and toxic.
I do not like that girl.

Kermit's an Easter egg.
Fun to look at
And search for.
The frog "escaped" today.
It took all of math and history
To track him down.

Question—Just how exactly
Does a frog escape
During math?

KAYLEY

Dear Ms. Graham,
    Our Egg Strategy rocks! I can't wait to see if we win.

I assigned Henry to listen to everyone else's strategies. It wasn't like we were going to copy them or anything. Aviva got all stressy about it, but it's called research, right? Then Aviva and Blake brainstormed some of our own ideas. I did both jobs, of course. That's what I hate about group projects. One person puts in all the work, and everyone else gets credit. *Sheesh.*

It was *my* idea. Hay. Sounds simple, right? We'll take a bunch of hay from Aviva's barn and pack our box full of it. In the very center we can place our egg. We'll win, for sure!

I invited my whole group over to my house this Saturday. We're going to do a trial run. There's no rule against that. There's this balcony outside my dad's study, and it's about the same height as the roof of the portables at school.

EMILY

Status: 😬
Dear Hope,

I'm trying really hard not to let Kayley and Aviva get me down. They're practically BUZZING about this egg drop thing. I bet Kayley's parents hired some kind of egg drop expert to coach them. It's NEVER a fair competition when Kayley's involved.

Kai and I made a mini-carrier for Kermit so that he can be out of his tank but not totally loose in the room. Kai's been bringing him over to our table group during class.

Sharon invited me to sit with her at lunch. Instead of

PB and J or turkey on wheat, she brings strange food. Like this thing she calls spanakopita (little triangles that look like pastries but have cheese and spinach inside). She let me try a bite. Normally, spinach makes me gag. But there were enough spices to cover it up.

I always used to think Sharon was weird. She's okay, I guess. I can't see being best friends with her or anything. But she's nice. Also, Cecilia has been stopping by to say "hi" on her way to the soccer field. That girl LIVES for soccer. It must be nice to love something so much.

Love and luck,
Emily

CECILIA

Hola Abuelita,

How are your English classes going? I wish you could come be a part of MY class. We're doing an egg drop. It's so cool! I guess it's science, but I can't believe this counts as school. It feels more like un juego to me.

It's practically a puzzle because eggs are so fragile. The outsides are as thin as paper, and even a tiny crack can send the insides leaking through. My team is smart, though—all A and B students (including me). We'll come up with a good idea, I'm sure.

I love to watch Mami's face when I bring her my grades. Good grades mean a good university, a good job someday, and a better future for us all. Sometimes I think our family is like that nursery rhyme where the egg falls off the wall and cracks. Mi familia is cracked into pieces, and we've landed so far apart from each other. I just hope I can put us back together again.

Oh, and I did put a sticky note on the fridge for Mami. "Una sonrisa es algo hermoso." Next thing I knew, Mami left one for me! "Your smile makes me smile." I was so proud of her for writing in English.

WORDS TO PRACTICE
conversations = *conversaciones*
puzzle = *rompecabezas*

Besos y abrazos,
Cecilia

HENRY

SCENE: *Ginormous richie-house, like something from a movie, with a remote-controlled gate around it, and tractor mowers for the lawn. Two kids standing on a balcony, throwing eggs off, two kids on the ground, checking them after they fall.*

KAYLEY: *(yells)* Are you ready?

HENRY: So actually, you don't have to yell. It's not like you're dropping the egg from the moon. We can hear you just fine if you talk.

KAYLEY: *(sighs)*

HENRY: See! I can even hear you sigh.

KAYLEY: I sighed extra loud to make a point.

BLAKE: Drop the egg already!

EGG: *Whoosh! (falls in box) Thud!*

KAYLEY: Wait! Don't open it. *(disappears from balcony, appears a few moments later out front with Aviva behind her)*

BLAKE: *(opens box, pulls out hay, dripping with yolk)* Oh, gross.

AVIVA: It didn't work.

HENRY: Maybe we packed the hay in there too tight.

KAYLEY: Don't stress, Aviva. This is why we're doing the trial run. I have another idea.

AVIVA: Yeah?

KAYLEY: Yeah. I think we can suspend the egg with my mother's pantyhose.

HENRY: Isn't that Kai's idea?

KAYLEY: I had it first! Two people can have the same idea, you know.

KIDS: *(silence)*

KAYLEY: I pinkie swear on my puppy's grave that I had the idea first. What? Are you calling me a liar?

KIDS: *(silence)*

HENRY: If I ever run for president, I want you to be my campaign manager.

AVIVA

Date: September 23

As long as I've known Kayley, she's *never* had a puppy. She never even pets Yoda when she comes over to my house. Out of the four of us, I was the only one who knew Kayley well enough to know that pinkie swearing on her puppy's grave meant she was lying. But I didn't say anything. Kayley would *never* forgive me if I called her out in front of everyone.

Kayley marched around cutting up a pair of her mother's hose, her face all twisted up like she'd eaten some sour yogurt.

I didn't feel right about it all afternoon. The thing was, when we dumped it off the balcony, the egg didn't break. But by the time we got home, my stomach hurt like *I* was the one who ate the sour yogurt.

BLAKE THE EGG WARS

CHAPTER 6

KAI

Hey, Frog!

I messed up. It was for a good reason, though, so maybe the bad and the good cancel each other out. Remember how I accidentally took Blake's journal a while back? Today I did it on purpose. I blame it all on my pencil.

The tip broke in the middle of Reflection Time. Blake sits next to the sharpener, and his drawings were practically right in front of me when I sharpened—I couldn't help seeing them. I didn't expect something so sad, though.

It made me worry for him. He's kind of a loner, you know? Most teachers don't like him much, because he causes problems. So I thought if I could figure out what was going on, then maybe I could help. That's why I took his journal home tonight.

I'm a nice guy. I can't see how this will hurt—Harry Potter broke all kinds of rules to save the world. That kind of thing works out okay in books.

BLAKE

KAI

Hey, Frog!

I'm pretty sure Blake's group is going to steal our egg strategy, but I can't tell anyone, because then it'll be obvious that I snagged his journal. Of course, stealing our strategy is wrong . . . but so is me taking his journal. Plus I saw way more important things in his journal than some stupid egg drop.

I went to talk to Blake today, but I couldn't figure out how to start. I packed a double lunch on purpose, and I tried to give some to him. I don't know how bad things are for him at home, but I figured extra food would help.

Only Blake already had a hot lunch. Maybe he gets it for free. Although they'd have to pay *me* to eat the cafeteria food. Meatloaf Surprise looks like something that should be flushed down a toilet, not set on a plate.

I decided the best thing to do is to send a letter to Ms. Graham. That way I can do it anonymously. I won't get in trouble . . . Blake will get help . . . it's the best solution I can figure out.

Ms. Graham,

Blake Benson needs help. I think he has problems at home. Someone should talk to him. A grown-up someone, not a kid someone.

—Anonymous

AViVA

Date: September 26

Ever since Kayley told Emily about La Ventana, Emily barely even *looks* at me. It's like I turned invisible. And now Kayley's stealing her team's egg drop idea, and I'm doing *nothing* to stop it. I wish I could fix things with Emily and maybe go back to walking to school together, but I can't ask her *now*.

I'm scared of seeing Tattoo Man again. I asked Ima if she would drive me to school for a while, but she said, "Exercise is good for you!" I wanted to say, "Yeah, but getting kidnapped is not!" I didn't, though. I want to tell her what happened, but I know how overprotective she and Aba are. If they think there's a bad guy in our neighborhood, they'll probably move us to Nebraska or never let me go outside. Instead, I've been riding my bike.

Only, yesterday after school I realized I'd forgotten my science book when I was already out unlocking my bike. I wheeled it back to the classroom with me and propped it against the wall. When I stepped inside, I saw Ms. Graham talking to Blake Benson. And he was crying. Not a sad crying but a *mad* crying. "Are you looking at my journal? I thought they were supposed to be private!"

And then he stormed past Kermit's tank and out the door. What was that about?

BLAKE

KAYLEY

Dear Ms. Graham,

I don't get the best grades, but I know I'm smart. My mother even had me tested for the gifted program. It's because I'm smart that I figure things out.

This is what I know: Kai took Blake's journal.

This is what I don't know: Why?

Here's *how* I know: I saw Kai trying to sneak a journal into the lockbox, and it was bugging me. I mean, we're allowed to take the journals home, so why the creeping around? I went over a couple of minutes later and pretended to be looking for my own journal. Really I was looking to see which journals were on top of the pile. Clever, huh? Blake's was right on top, but I had to dig deep to find Kai's.

And what makes this situation even weirder is that Blake is going around telling everyone that YOU read his journal. Not that this surprises me. Did I call that . . . or what? He must've written something really juicy if you talked to him about it. It drives me bananas not to know what it is.

Why does everyone care so much about what Blake is writing? He's not that interesting, believe me. I sit across from the guy every day and he hardly says a word. And half the time he's drawing frogs or other equally disgusting creatures.

Give me a day or two, Ms. Graham. I'll figure this out.

PS Can't WAIT for the Egg Drop!!!! We're gonna rock it!

Dear Ms. Graham,

You have a Thief in your class.

Someone IS reading the journals (besides you, that is).

I'm not going to rat him out. I just want to make sure you know.

—Anonymous

BLAKE

SHARON

Classroom lecture, Graham-style.
Normally Ms. Graham's eyes
Smile all the time,
But today her eyes are not
Crinkling in the corners,
And her mouth is flat.

She sits on her stool to tell us that
Journals are private
Trust is sacred
Rumors are flying
And SHE would never-ever-never-ever-never-ever
    violate privacy.
And she hopes WE would never-ever-never-ever-never-ever
    violate privacy either.

It is up to US, as a class, to mend this.

KAI

Hey, Frog!
    It's kind of hard not to feel guilty, even though I think I did
the right thing. I didn't mean for Blake to accuse Ms. Graham of
reading his journal. My face got blazing hot when Ms. Graham

explained that she'd gotten an anonymous note to talk to a student. I stared hard at my fingernails.

We're going to vote on how to store the journals. That's kind of a relief—I sort of regret snagging it in the first place, because now I'm worried about Blake, but I don't know what to do about it.

I tried to talk my egg group into changing our strategy. I don't want our group and Blake's group to do the exact same thing. What if Ms. Graham thinks *our* group is the one that stole the idea? But no one else wants to change. They all think the nylon will work, and I can't tell them why I want to swap it out.

HENRY

SCENE: *Students preparing to vote. Handsome, brilliant, and athletic Henry is passing around slips of paper for voting. He's ripped like Mr. Olympia, so his muscles bulge every time he moves his arms.*

MS. GRAHAM: Henry is passing around your voting slips. I realize some students feel like their journals are not entirely private, so we'll vote on how best to store them.

HENRY: *(whispers)* Kermit for president! Vote for the frog.

KAYLEY: *(whispers)* Shut up.

MS. GRAHAM: I will remind you of your options. Option number one—keep the journals locked up and I hold the key.

Option number two—keep them locked and nominate a student to hold the key.

HENRY: *(whispers)* Ooh, that one. Vote for Henry as the key holder. *(taps Aviva on the shoulder)* Look at this face. Doesn't it scream Trustworthy?

MS. GRAHAM: Henry—I don't believe the task of passing out slips of paper requires talking.

HENRY: *(freezes in place with winning smile)* Sorry, Ms. Graham.

MS. GRAHAM: Option number three—keep your journals in your desks or backpacks. Option number four—you each choose individually either to keep it in your desk or backpack or to keep it in the lockbox, whatever makes you most comfortable.

HENRY: *(sits down quietly like the good, responsible student he is)*

MS. GRAHAM: Please vote on your slips of paper, and then fold them in half before they are collected.

HENRY: *(holds back what he really wants to say, which is "Option number five—order takeout for the whole class. Curly fries and chocolate shakes for everyone!")*

Five minutes pass. Camera zooms in on tally written on chalkboard. Option number four wins.

CHAPTER 7

BLAKE   EGG DROP

To Break or Not to Break

SHARON

I find it suspicious
That out of a thousand and one
Different ways to package an egg,
Two of our groups in class had the
Exact. Same. Idea.

Dear Ms. Graham—

These assignments are fun, but people are stealing ideas.
Just saying.

—Anonymous

CECILIA

Hola Abuelita,

You'd be so proud, Abuelita! Our egg didn't break, and neither did the eggs from three other groups. Ms. Graham is having an "Egg-Off!" In order to find a true winner, she's going to give us each a box of supplies. She'll put us in different rooms and give us an hour to design another egg drop container. If more than one egg doesn't break, the winner will be the container that's the lightest weight.

Here's what we've got in our box (I'm going to give you all the Spanish translations):

string = *cuerda*

plastic bag = *bolsa de plástico*

balloons = *globos*

glue = *pegamento*

duct tape = *cinta adhesiva*

cotton balls = *bolas de algodón*

potato chips = *papas fritas*

small apple = *manzana pequeña*

100 straws = *cien popotes*

Silly Putty = *plastilina*

a roll of toilet paper = *un rollo de papel de baño*

scissors = *tijeras*

gift bag = *bolsa de regalo*

popcorn = *palomitas de maiz*

box (we can use the box itself) = *caja*

Our team got right to work, making a parachute out of the trash bag and string. Then we tied the parachute to the gift bag handles. We wrapped the egg in toilet paper and set it inside the gift bag. We brought Kermit over to our work area for good luck. I can't wait until we test it later this afternoon! Wish me luck, Abuelita!

> Besos y abrazos,
> Cecilia

HENRY

SCENE: *Kayley, Aviva, Henry, and Blake sit in a small teacher workroom, trying to rig a container. Kayley is shrieking and running around the room. Apparently she thinks this is helpful.*

KAYLEY: *(shrieks)* Focus! We only have thirty more minutes!

BLAKE: *(ignores her, tapes straws together in a structure with a pocket in the center)*

KAYLEY: I can't believe she's making us do this here! At school! With no time to prep!

HENRY: *(creates a duct tape–balloon ball)* Yeah. We can't even cheat! *(pauses)* We actually have a stellar team, I hope you know. We can do this.

KAYLEY: Stop messing around, guys! We're running out of time!

AVIVA: *(looks up at Kayley briefly, then goes back to blowing up balloons)*

HENRY: *(speaks calmly)* Kayley, you're shrieking.

KAYLEY: Because we're running out of time!

HENRY: I'm not sure if you've noticed, Kayley, but we've got two awesome ideas here.

KAYLEY: But we only have one egg! We might break it by accident, and then we'd LOSE!

HENRY: You're still shrieking. No shrieking.

KAYLEY: *(shrieks)* I am not shrieking!

AVIVA: We can practice with this apple, maybe put it in the center. And see if it bruises?

BLAKE: Great idea. It's heavier than the egg, but it's so little that it's close.

HENRY: Don't forget we're going for lightest here. *(He wedges the apple into the center of his balloon–duct tape ball and throws it against a wall. It drifts down.)*

BLAKE: Dude! Yours is genius!

HENRY: Why, thank you. I try. But yours is pretty genius too. *(He takes unbruised apple out of center and wedges it inside the straw structure, then drops it. It bounces lightly.)*

KAYLEY: *(not shrieking)* Wow.

HENRY: Kayley! You're not shrieking! Congratulations! Your prize is a bag of chips. *(throws a bag of chips at her)*

BLAKE: I don't even care if we win! That was the funnest hour of school in my whole life.

KAYLEY: *(crunches potato chips with a small smile)*

AVIVA

Date: September 29

For the first time in my life, I felt sorry for Kayley. She *totally* didn't get it. The rest of us were having so much fun playing around and creating new ideas, and she missed all that. The only thing she could think about was whether we would win and what kind of grade she'd get. All of a sudden, that seemed really sad to me. Maybe it's kind of hard to be Kayley Barrette.

Sometimes I feel jealous about all the cool clothes she has, and the big house and pool and how she seems so confident all the time. But I am *so glad* I'm not her. I much prefer to be me. Of course, I wouldn't mind being me *and* having a pool.

KAI

Hey, Frog!

Whoop! That was tight! The time pressure turned up the heat and we were all on fire! Our parachute drifted down so slow it looked like a piece of dandelion fluff. When we peeked inside our bag, the egg was good as new!

I have to say that the parachute idea was brilliant. And simple. Way better than nylons.

Three out of the four Egg-Off teams had unbroken eggs at the end. But when Ms. Graham lugged out a big old grocery fruit scale, ours came in the lightest. *Yes!!!* I thought about doing my big brother's classic slam-dunk victory dance down the aisle, but I didn't want to rub it in anyone's face, so I just smiled. The team with the balloons and duct tape came in second. I think the duct tape weighed it down.

Nobody seemed to care who won, though, and that was nice.

PS The Land of Stories by Chris Colfer is *amazing*.

CHAPTER 8

BLAKE

CECILIA

Hola Abuelita,

Ooh! I've got vocabulary words for you. Know what "physical fitness" means? It's a way to say how in shape you are. Every morning, before we sit in our seats, we run. Around and around the track, four times. By the time we're done, my legs have turned to rubber and my heart is beating right out of my chest, but I'm ready to learn. It clears my brain somehow. I love the feeling of wind brushing my face and skating through my hair.

All my soccer practice makes me fast. I don't want to be a show-off, but I can't help pushing myself as hard as I can. Emily cheers for me each time I loop the track. "Go, Cecilia!" she calls. This makes me embarrassed, but in a good way. When it's her turn, I'll cheer for her too.

I wish you could meet the kids in my class, Abuelita! I just know you'd love them.

WORDS TO PRACTICE
rubber = *hule*
embarrassed = *avergonzado*
brain = *cerebro*

Besos y abrazos,
Cecilia

KAYLEY

Dear Ms. Graham,

Who came up with this physical fitness program? It's biased. How fast we run and how many pull-ups we do—how does that tell us if we're "fit" or not?

I'm not pointing this out for myself. I'm one of the faster girls, and I can do five pull-ups, which isn't bad. I'm thinking of Aviva, though. She's super-fit. She rides horses and carries these ginormous bales of hay, but the girl can't run. As long as she tries her best, she should get an A for effort.

Although I guess you could make the same argument for someone like Blake. He can't spell, but if he tries hard, should he get an A for effort? I don't know. He's the fastest boy runner. Honestly, it doesn't look like he's even trying. It looks like it's as easy as breathing.

KAI

Hey, Frog!

People think boys should be good at sports. My brother, Thomas, sure is. I guess I sort of look like I *could* be. I'm pretty tall and a stretchy kind of skinny. And I do own a ridiculous number of Lakers T-shirts/sweatshirts/caps. Thomas and I have this deal, that if we shoot hoops, we also do a round of Rubik's Cube or chess, to make it fair. He serves me up in basketball, and I return the favor with a game of chess.

Not to brag, but brain games are my thing. I can solve the Rubik's Cube in under a minute. I can do it behind my back in two, and hanging upside down from the monkey bars in ninety seconds. Truth is, I like *watching* sports more than playing them. I like to yell at the television and eat popcorn and drink soda. So . . . running is not my favorite. I'm cool with having my muscles burn and feeling sweaty and sinking a few baskets now and then, but I'll take books over laps any day.

After today's running torture, we were sitting in our seats, sweaty and out of breath, when Kayley proposed a measure for class council. She said we should make our daily runs into relay races. That way no one would feel embarrassed about their speed, and she said our table groups would even us out. At first I was suspicious, and I figured she was just trying to find another way to beat out our team. But even though she and Blake are fast, Aviva's pretty slow.

Emily and I discussed, and we both agreed that relay races are the way to go. If Ms. Graham still wants us to run four laps, we can each circle four times *before* the handoff. Ms. Graham didn't veto either. *Yes!!!!* Relays approved.

SHARON

When Ms. Graham blew the whistle
To start our relay,
I pumped my legs so fast

That I could hardly feel them.
Like they were disconnected from my body.

Aviva grabbed her baton
A few seconds before me.
I passed her right off,
My lungs burning for air
And the track dust fluffing around my feet.

But then as I neared the end of my fourth lap,
Aviva finished her third,
Handing her baton off
To Blake's outstretched palm.

Maybe it was the heat.
Or the lack of oxygen to my brain.
Did Aviva really just cheat?
She doesn't seem the cheating kind.
Did she get confused? Miscount her laps?

All I know is she turned her head,
With a face as happy as summer.
Kayley put her arm around Aviva's shoulder
And whispered in her ear.
I watched as Aviva's smile melted.

HENRY

SCENE: *Class lecture. Students are hot and sweaty after the run. The room is stinking up like old socks in a microwave. Ms. Graham makes everyone set their chairs up in a big circle.*

MS. GRAHAM: Today I was impressed with someone's character. One of our students, who will remain unnamed, accidentally ran three laps instead of four. This person didn't realize until after they'd handed the baton off. If they hadn't said anything, I wouldn't have known. But they did. This person came up to me in private and shared the mistake.

KAYLEY: *(nudges Aviva quietly)*

AVIVA: *(blushes)*

MS. GRAHAM: I want to compliment this student for his or her character. I know that there are times when people in this room have not been entirely honest and trustworthy. I won't point fingers, but you know who you are.

HENRY: *(dripping sweat like a broken faucet and glaring pointedly at Kayley)*

KAYLEY: *(stares straight ahead, innocently)*

MS. GRAHAM: I'd like you all to journal about honesty today. Reflect on yourself. Reflect on your personal choices. I challenge you to be as honest as you can. Bottom line, you get to choose what kind of person you want to be. Make choices that make you proud.

STUDENTS: *(quiet, thinking)*

HENRY: *(trying not to sweat on Aviva, who is sitting next to him and still blushing)*

AViVA

Date: October 5

Ms. Graham gave us this huge speech today, and it's *because of me.* Once I realized I'd screwed up, there's *no way* I could have stopped myself from telling Ms. Graham. Kayley said it was no big deal, that it wasn't like I cheated *on purpose.* But knowing that I cheated started chewing up my insides, and I had to tell.

Ms. Graham acted like I was so honest and everything, but I'm really not. I didn't tell anyone that Kayley stole the nylon idea or that she lied about her pinkie promise. Yesterday, Kayley told Emily-the-vegetarian that the school pizza sauce had meat in it (which I know is a *complete* lie), but I didn't say anything. Doesn't that make me a liar too? Probably.

When Ms. Graham talked about choosing what kind-of-a-person we want to be, of course this made me think about Emily. I know it hurts her feelings that I'm hanging out with Kayley. I don't mean for it to, but I *need* Kayley to be my friend for next year.

Plus I think Kayley's been a little nicer recently. I'm pretty sure she suggested the relay race for me. She's an okay friend.

I just wish she wouldn't be mean to Emily. And I wish it was easier for me to stand up to her. Why can't I go back to being friends with both of them? *Why* do I have to pick?

EMILY

Status: 🌑

Dear Hope,

I felt sick to my stomach after what Kayley told me. I had no idea that the school sauce had meat in it. I've been off meat for three years now. Ever since Dad did that article on the way cows and chickens are treated. I'll never buy school lunch again!

I went to the bathroom to splash water on my face. I know it's ridiculous to cry about something like pizza. But I've never been any good at holding back tears. Cecilia and Sharon were washing their hands in the sink. They sort of looked at each other, then looked at me. I'm pretty sure they could tell I was upset. But they didn't make it weird by asking a bunch of questions. Instead they just walked with me back to class.

Ms. Graham assigned us to write about honesty. If I'm being honest, I'm pretty lonely. Dad's gone . . . always. Mom's busy painting, and since the house is empty except for us, we don't do "sit-down" dinners anymore. I mostly eat on the couch with the television on. My friends are disappearing. Sharon and Cecilia are nice enough, but it's not the same.

Honesty is a complicated thing. I can't just go up to Aviva and

Kayley and tell them how much they're hurting me, because too bad for me, they DON'T CARE! I can't tell Mom, because she'll just worry and be sad, and then I'll have to cheer her up again. I can't tell Dad, because . . . he's never here. So what's the point of being honest if there's no one to be honest with?

Love and luck,
Emily

KAYLEY

Dear Ms. Graham,

I'm an honest person. In fact, I'm more honest than most people. I only lie when I have a good reason to lie. Just so you know, when I told Emily the pizza had meat sauce, that wasn't a lie. It was a joke. There's a difference.

And the egg drop? There's no rule against researching what works and doesn't work. Keeping our ears open is really no different from Googling on the internet. We were just being resourceful. Plus we wound up having the Egg-Off anyway, so it's all good.

I cannot believe Aviva went up and confessed to you, Ms. Graham. That girl is too honest. If she farted and someone smelled it, she'd probably fess up instead of pretending she didn't know where it came from. Still . . . it's hard not to respect her for that.

Ms. Graham, if you like honesty so much, you'll get honesty. I will be 100% honest for the rest of the day! See? I can be like Aviva too.

CHAPTER 9

SHARON

Kayley has the special ability
To take anything she hears
And twist it
Torque it
Mangle it
For her own purposes.

Like this honesty thing . . .
Today she straight-out
Told Emily she'd outgrown her.
Told Blake he needed a tutor.
And pointed out the stain on Aviva's skirt.

"What? I was just being honest."
I heard that sorry excuse
For a jab
Spill out of her mouth
Way too many times.
Sometimes that girl
Makes me want to scream.

HENRY

SCENE: *Ms. Graham writes the following on the board: "Being honest is not an excuse to be mean." Students brace themselves for a lecture.*

MS. GRAHAM: *(perches on stool)* What do you all think I mean by that statement? *(points to her socks, which are decorated with frogs)* Like, for example, what if I asked you all what you think about my socks?

STUDENTS: *(raising hands)*

MS. GRAHAM: Don't answer that quite yet. Because if you were honest, some of you would say that this pattern is too babyish for a teacher in a fifth-grade classroom. Some of you would say that you don't like it. But I bet that most of you would stop yourselves and think that making a comment like that might hurt my feelings.

HENRY: *(whispers to Kayley)* So if I ask you whether I'm the funniest, most entertaining seat partner ever, just be honest and admit that I'm growing on you.

KAYLEY: *(scootches away)* You're definitely the most irritating seat partner ever. And that's honest.

HENRY: *(modestly)* Thank you. I try.

MS. GRAHAM: Remember, *you* get to decide what kind of person you want to be. Let me ask you this—are there any options that would protect my feelings and be truthful at the same time?

EMILY: Your socks are creative.

SHARON: And colorful.

HENRY: And frog-tastic!

STUDENTS: *(laugh)*

HENRY: They're frog-alicious. And frog-erful. They're practically a frog-a-rama!

MS. GRAHAM: Yes! That's a perfect way to both protect someone's feelings *and* be honest.

AVIVA: I really *do* like your socks.

SEVERAL STUDENTS: *(laugh)*

AVIVA: What? *(looks around)* I do. *(blushes)*

MS. GRAHAM: Thank you for sharing, Aviva. I like them too.

HENRY: Me too.

AVIVA: *(smiles at her feet)*

EMILY

Status: 😡
Dear Hope,

    I cannot believe Kayley had the nerve to say she had "outgrown" me! Like I'm a pair of too-tight pants? Well, guess what?

I've outgrown her too. That "being honest is not an excuse to be mean" lecture was TOTALLY directed at Kayley. I'm pretty sure everyone knew it. Everyone except maybe Kayley? Clearly she's "decided" what kind of person she wants to be, and that's a JERK.

I decided that I forgive Ms. Graham for not letting me change table groups. As awful as it is to be in Kayley's class now, I can't imagine how it'd be if we were in the same table group. I hardly ever say this word, but . . . I think I hate her. And I definitely hate that she took Aviva away from me.

I can't hate Aviva, even when I try to. I just miss her. She practically let me move in with her for the first couple of weeks after the divorce. That was while Dad packed his things and Mom filled up the bathtub with tears. I can never forget that Aviva was there for me then.

I'm glad Aviva spoke up about the socks. She loves anything about nature. When we studied snails in second grade, I swear she got obsessed. She thought snails were the cutest things ever. Seriously. She drew pictures of them to tape up all over her room. I remember crawling around in her backyard with empty spreadable butter containers. We poked holes with pencils in the lids. We picked up snails with our hands.

Personally, I never thought snails were cute, not even the babies—I just acted like I did. I guess that's a lie too, kind of, but I was just trying to be a good friend. If Ms. Graham asked me, I'd say that's the kind of person I want to be—a good friend.

I wish things weren't so broken with Aviva these days. Maybe she's like one of those animals that change colors based on their environment? To camouflage themselves? Geckos and chameleons do that. And some frogs change their colors to avoid getting gobbled up by predators. Although I don't think Aviva *wants* to change? Maybe she thinks she has to morph herself to survive. Not that Kayley would eat her up. Or would she?

Love and luck,
Emily

PS I've been eating lunch with Sharon almost every day. She's definitely growing on me. Sharon's like an anti-chameleon. She *doesn't* change for her environment even when she REALLY should. Sometimes that makes her seem weird. And sometimes that makes her seem cool. For sure it makes her reliable. Cecilia is nice too. When I'm with them both, I don't have to try to be fun or cheerful. I can just be me.

KAYLEY

Dear Ms. Graham,

You said we get to choose what kind of person we want to be. You're right. I *choose* to be the kind of person who stands up for what I believe. I know part of your "being honest is not an excuse to be mean" lecture was pointed at me, but sometimes people need to hear the truth. I say it like it is. My mother does too. She shares her opinion and if it makes people mad, well then, too bad for them.

Speaking of which, I have to stand up for the privacy of our

journals. Today I wrote Kai a note for his mailbox with my left
hand to disguise my writing.

> Kai,
>   You're a thief. I know you took someone else's
> journal. You're the reason for that whole honesty
> lecture. It was a pain.
>   —Anonymous

PS Ms. Graham, I don't know why I keep writing these journal
entries to you. Since I'm pretty much not letting this journal
out of my sight except at recess, I don't think you could possibly
be reading it. But somehow it feels right to keep addressing it
to you.

KAi

Hey, Frog!

I got this note in my box today, calling me a thief. And I
thought, "Here we go." I'm not one to walk away from anything,
and even though this whole journal thing was an honest mistake at first, I know I've got to own it.

I tried to catch up with Blake today . . . so I could explain,
but I took too long gathering my homework folder, and before
I knew it, he was halfway down the street. I called to him a
couple of times, but he had his earbuds in, and I guess he was
listening to music or something, so he didn't hear me. Then the

dude walked so fast! I couldn't keep up and I was practically running.

All of a sudden he disappeared around a corner . . . and in an okay neighborhood. (????) So maybe I'm wrong about all this. His journal made it look like he was really poor or something. Maybe he and his mom are renting a room.

I guess the best thing is to be nice to the guy. Last year our teacher read *Wonder* out loud to get us talking about being kind to each other no matter what our differences are. I thought I'd hate it, because I'm a fantasy and sci-fi guy. But when she got to that part where the kids and Auggie are in the woods, I had to put my face down on my desk so no one would see me crying and think I was a wuss. And then I borrowed *Wonder* from the library and read it at home a whole mess of times. I don't know why I liked it so much. I guess it just makes me want to be a better person.

PS I know Blake's really into Kermit. I could take him to visit my parents' university. There's a whole biology wing—I bet he'd love it.

BLAKE

CHAPTER 10

HENRY

SCENE: *Ms. Graham loses her marbles.*

MS. GRAHAM: We'll be changing seats and table groups for the next two days while I try a new teaching technique.

STUDENTS: *(half groan and half cheer)*

HENRY: Finally! Now I can try my material on someone who'll actually crack a smile.

KAYLEY: Finally! Now I can actually focus without being interrupted every three seconds.

MS. GRAHAM: This will only be for two days, so don't get too excited or too upset. This morning, when I called you each up to my desk for an assessment, I asked if you could whistle. All of those students who were given an orange sticker with the word "Whistler" in black letters, please place this sticker on your shirt now.

STUDENTS: *(rumbling)*

MS. GRAHAM: For the next two days, we'll call this group of high achievers the Whistlers. At this time, I'd like all the Whistlers to move their desks to the front of the room. And all the Non-Whistlers, move your desks to the back of the room.

STUDENTS: *(confused rumbling)*

MS. GRAHAM: Quiet, please. I know this seems strange, but new research is showing that on average, Whistlers are capable of accessing a greater percentage of their brains. If I keep all the Whistlers at the front of the room, maybe the Non-Whistlers can learn from them. We are trying to maximize learning here.

HENRY: *(whispers)* Uh, what? That makes zero sense. Neither I nor my sister can whistle, and we're Taiwanese. If some percentage of people use higher brainpower, it's us Asians. We rule the world!

KAYLEY: Shhh!

HENRY: *(whispers)* No, seriously. You watch TV, right? Have you ever heard of an Asian who wasn't brilliant?

KAYLEY: You mean besides you?

HENRY: Hey! That was funny! You're getting the hang of this.

KAYLEY: Shut up. Plus that's a stereotype anyway. You're being racist.

HENRY: I'm allowed to make jokes about my own minority group. Didn't you read the handbook? Aviva sometimes jokes about not eating bacon, because she's Jewish, but I can't. It'd be offensive if I did. You can joke about rich people. That's how it works. I'm allowed to joke about the superior intelligence of my people.

MS. GRAHAM: Kayley and Henry. Please hold your conversation. Kayley, I'm assuming you're explaining this concept to Henry, since it does sometimes take Non-Whistlers longer to understand.

HENRY: *(whispers)* Is that a joke?

MS. GRAHAM: Non-Whistlers will need more time on assignments, so I'll be releasing the Whistlers first for recess and lunch and after school.

HENRY: What about people who can raise one eyebrow at a time? *(raising right eyebrow)* I bet we use a higher percentage of brainpower too. Or how about people who can sneeze with their eyes open? *(comedic pause)* Because my neighbor can. For real.

MS. GRAHAM: *(yelling)* Non-Whistlers! Focus!

SHARON: *(raises hand)*

MS. GRAHAM: Sharon, you'll have to wait. You're a Non-Whistler. I'm going to be taking questions from Whistlers first. If you listen carefully, Non-Whistlers, your questions will be answered.

HENRY: *(groans silently)*

EMILY

Status: 😔

Dear Hope,

I can't believe I was beginning to like Ms. Graham. I thought she actually cared about us. But apparently, I was wrong. I'm a Non-Whistler, and she's being SO mean to us! I hid in the bathroom at recess to practice my whistling, but I can still only blow air.

I hate it when I think people are cool and then they change up on me. It feels like a trick. Like what Kayley and Aviva have done to me. (It doesn't help that they're both Whistlers.) Or like the birthday when I turned six and Mom decided to go healthy and make me a watermelon cake. She seriously stuck candles in a slab of watermelon and thought I'd be happy. Or the divorce . . . for obvious reasons.

But Life does that to me all the time. Sticks its tongue out at me and wags it. "You thought things were gonna be okay? Nope—just kidding. Life's gonna suck again."

Discouraged,
Emily

(I can't even put on my fake-happy face right now.)

CECILIA

Hola Abuelita,

I'm so glad I have friends outside Ms. Graham's class. The other teachers aren't doing the Whistler thing (thank goodness), so I can forget about this annoying classroom drama at lunch.

I don't understand Ms. Graham. Shouldn't she be pairing us up so the Whistlers can help the Non-Whistlers learn? Some things are a mystery to me.

Abuelita, guess what? I'm going to join a soccer team outside of school. Some of the girls who play at lunch are on a YMCA team. There are practices on Mondays and Wednesdays at four-thirty at Melbourne Park. Mami doesn't get off work until five, but it's close enough to our apartment to walk. Can't wait to start!

Today I dove for a save in the high corner and blocked it! Someday you've got to see me play goalie. Maybe Mami can take a video on her phone and send it to you. Te extraño mucho.

<u>WORDS TO PRACTICE</u>
YMCA = Do you remember going there on weekends for their tiny tot soccer, Abuelita?

Besos y abrazos,
Cecilia

KAYLEY

Dear Ms. Graham,

Today you made me laugh! No offense, but you're a little batty for giving Whistlers first choice on everything. Although I agree that we needed more order in the classroom. And the whole "take it to the class" thing is a big time-waster. Don't get me wrong—it's nice to have freedom and responsibilities and all that, but not everyone's as mature as I am.

So I'm glad you came up with a system. It's simple: Whistlers Rule! Non-Whistlers Drool! You should observe our next recess, though, so you can see how some of those Non-Whistlers are behaving. Like poor sports! Just because they can't whistle. *Sheesh!*

BLAKE

SHARON

Sometimes I wonder
Why I always have to be the one
To speak up.
Does no one else have a voice?
Does no one else see the unfairness?
Does no one else notice
The way the Whistler stupidity
Pits kid against kid
So easily?

Although I guess
When you look at history
(Which is, by the way, the *point*—obviously)
Grown-ups
Have done much, much worse.
If that's the point, though,
To show us what we can do
To each other
So easily, so quickly,
Then maybe it's best if I *don't* say
A single thing at all.

AVIVA

Date: October 18

Am I the only one that thinks this Whistler thing is a metaphor? I mean, Ms. Graham has us reading *The Diary of a Young Girl* by Anne Frank, and we're learning about segregation in history. The scary thing is how much everyone has gotten into it. Some of the boys started a water fountain fight at recess. I don't think Ms. Graham realizes how fast things can get out of control.

I brought Kermit to sit with me at my desk today. I watched him breathe, and that calmed me down and helped me think. Should I say something? I always get stressed about speaking up, like maybe I'm wrong or something. I usually just wait around and eventually someone says what I wanted to say. I guess I let someone else be my voice.

Ms. Graham set up the class council. Now's the time to use it. We need to vote this Whistler thing away. This is uber-ly stressful.

Maybe I *should* speak up now.

KAI

Hey, Frog!

Kayley's getting on my nerves. She thinks she's such hot stuff because she's a Whistler. Our teams are sort of rivals anyway, what with them stealing our first Egg Drop idea, and all that tension between Emily and her.

Girls are so mean to each other sometimes. And Kayley's walking around like she's Draco Malfoy or some Percy Jackson demigod. Emily's been sniffling all morning, and her eyes are lobster red.

I'm done.

Someone's gotta say something. It might just have to be me.

KAYLEY

Dear Ms. Graham,

I can't believe Kai! Who does he think he is? Cornering me like that! Talking so loud that half the school could hear?

Well, I stayed totally calm.

I told him in a very soft voice so only he could hear that I knew he'd stolen Blake's journal, so who was he to talk! That I could tell on him if I wanted to. That made him stop talking real fast.

SHARON

Aviva surprised me today.
She dropped a note
Into Ms. Graham's mailbox as she walked by
When we filed back in from recess,
Sweaty and breathing hard.
Ms. Graham had taped the note
Squarely on the front of her desk.
"I would like to propose a new law," it read.
"That every student is treated equally."

Aviva sat in her seat,
Her cheeks the color of pomegranates.
I wanted to hug her.
Why couldn't she own her idea?
It was a good one.
Still . . . I'm proud of her for speaking up.
And I'm proud of me for holding back
Just a little bit
So she could be heard.

CHAPTER 11

To my esteemed fifth-grade students,

Thank you for putting up with my Whistler Experiment. Your class met the challenge faster than most. I was waiting for someone to point out the error of my ways. I'd like to make it clear that I've found <u>ZERO</u> scientific research about whistling relating to intelligence. I wanted to pick something completely meaningless and link it to preferential treatment.

As you all know from our history lessons, people have not always been treated equally. Our task is to learn the lessons from our past so that we don't repeat the same mistakes, and to speak up when we see an injustice.

Current social issues will be the focus of our next unit. I expect you will all rise to the challenge. Before we begin, however, I believe we have some repair work to do.

I would like each of you to write at least two letters to people in this class. I hope that this will build bridges.

Please include at least one affirmation in each letter. (An affirmation is something nice.) For example, I'd like to affirm you all by saying that I appreciate you—your creative ideas, your distinct personalities, and the way you've embraced your class jobs and assignments.

Sincerely,

Ms. Graham

Dear Blake,

Do you want to hang out sometime? We could skateboard or something. Or we could build something cool for the frog habitat.

I think you're a great runner and artist.

From Kai

Dear Kayley,

Are we cool?

So you know where I'm coming from—I don't like it when I see people get hurt feelings. Emily's all right. You all used to be friends, right? Seems like she shouldn't have to feel bad all the time.

Your affirmation—I liked your relay race idea.

From Kai

Dear Aviva,

I really miss the way we used to hang out and laugh about stuff. I'm not sure what happened? You will always be one of my best friends.

From Emily 😌

———

Dear Ms. Graham,

I love your frog decorations, and I think you're a good teacher. Did you just happen to have all those frog decorations at home? Or are you buying them for our class? Did you like frogs before Kermit? I'm curious about this.

From Emily 😊

———

Dear Kai,

Yes, we can skateboard. Or build something for Kermit. That will be fun.

Blake

Dear Kermit,

I wish you could talk. I'd love to hear what you have to say.
Affirmation: You're the most frog-errific frog I've ever known.

Henry

PS I made you a mailbox out of an empty tissue box. Seems only
fair that you get letters too.

Dear Kayley,

You run fast.

Blake

Dear Blake,

Thank you. I am a fast runner. So are you. You are a good
artist. I think you should take professional drawing classes. You
had some good ideas for the Egg-Off too.

From Kayley

Dear Kai,

People don't have to stay friends with the same kids forever, you know. It is possible to move on. That's life.

From Kayley

PS We need to talk.

Dear Kayley,

When? Where?

From Kai

Dear Kai,

Lunch recess. Tomorrow.

From Kayley

Dear Kayley,

A true comedian needs to be able to make anyone laugh. At first you never smiled, not even with my best material, but now I get a smile like 25% of the time. My goal is to get it to 50% by the end of the year. Wish me luck.

From Henry

What do you think, Ms. Graham?

                                    —Blake

———

Dear Emily,

I'm sorry things have been so weird.

I miss you too.

                                    From Aviva

———

Dear Henry,

Good luck! You'll need it if you think you're going to make me smile 50% of the time. You ARE funny (that's your affirmation), but in an irritating itchy-bug-bite way. I don't laugh because I'm trying not to encourage you.

                                    From Kayley

Dear Emily,

I've really liked eating lunch with you this year. You are one of those people who are always nice.

From Sharon

Dear Blake,

Thank you for your drawing. It's perfect. I'd love it if you can sketch me a large one, maybe on one of those extra poster boards? I'd like to hang it in the classroom as a reminder for everyone.

Also, I just want you to know that I notice your kindness and caring for Kermit. I see you checking on the habitat, making sure there's clean water and food. Kermit appreciates you too.

Sincerely,

Ms. Graham

Dear Kai,

How do you read so fast? Every time I turn around, you're reading another book. Also, you're brave to stand up to Kayley.

From Cecilia

Dear Blake,

Dude! You are the best artist ever in the history of the world. You're gonna be famous. When you're a millionaire, remember I said that. Of course I'm gonna be a millionaire famous director too, so maybe we'll play golf or something.

From Henry

Dear Henry

Ha ha, dude!

Can't wait to be rich.

Blake

Dear Sharon,

I can't believe we've been at the same school since kindergarten and we've been eating lunch together since September, but we haven't ever really gotten together outside of school. Maybe we can hang out sometime.

From Emily 😊

Dear Cecilia,

My mom says I was born with a book in my hand. If you ever need a recommendation for a good read, let me know.

From Kai

Dear Emily,

It's been a pleasure teaching you all.

And thank you for your interest in my extensive (and rapidly growing) collection of frog posters, socks, figurines, earrings, and decorative coffee cups. They are all new purchases for me, although I prefer to buy "gently used" when I can. Now I've got a classroom theme.

Can you stay after school today? I've been meaning to find a time to chat with you.

Sincerely,
Ms. Graham

SHARON

Not that I'm counting,
But I got one letter in my box today.
I wrote six.
Still . . .
I have to say that Emily's letter
Is worth a thousand.

———

Dear Emily,

Want to hang out on Friday after school?

From Sharon

EMILY

Status: 😕

Dear Hope,

Ms. Graham freaked me out by having me stay after school, but all she wanted was to ask how things were going *socially*. Only what could I do, tell Ms. Graham what an awful person Kayley had become? And about Aviva being a chameleon? No way. That'd feel like tattling.

So I just sort of shrugged and said this year has been different from what I thought. But that I was okay. She patted my back and just said, "Sometimes what we *think* we want doesn't wind up being what we actually want."

It took me a moment to figure out what she meant. But then I got it—exactly what happened with me and my table group. Now I'm glad I'm not sitting with Aviva and Kayley.

And she smiled and said her door was always open if I need to talk.

And that was it.

> Love and luck,
> Emily

PS After Aviva and I sent letters to each other, I sort of thought things would change. But she's still not talking to me or hanging out with me at school. Maybe she only wants to be nice to me when Kayley can't see?

PPS Sharon invited me over on Friday. I think I'll go. Why not?

KAI

Hey, Frog!

I was stressing out when Kayley confronted me about Blake's journal. I almost fessed up, but then I decided if I'm going to fess up, it should be to Blake, not to her. Plus there's no way she could know I took it on purpose. But then the guilt got to me. I wanted to own this and I haven't yet, not really. I've got to find a way to make this right.

> Dear Blake,
>
> Let's hang out at the park after school tomorrow. Bring your skateboard.
>
> I'm decorating the front of my journal with stripes because guess what? Our journals look exactly the same, and I keep grabbing yours instead of mine. My bad—won't happen again.
>
> From
>
> Kai

After I finished Blake's note, I felt much better. I didn't make it sound like a big deal or anything, and it really isn't. I can't wait to hang out—I'll stuff my backpack full of snacks (I've got homemade caramel corn) and let him take as much as he wants. Plus the park is huge and sort of woodsy. I bet we could gather stuff for our habitat.

BLAKE

CHAPTER 12

To my esteemed fifth-grade students,

We are moving toward our unit on current social issues. I'd like us to all stretch beyond our individual lives and look at the big picture.

Today your teams will begin discussing social issues. Each team will have two weeks to select a social issue as an area of focus for our next project. Think of something that matters to the world. Think about what kind of impact you'd like to have. If you had a magic wand, what would you change?

I've broken down the steps to completing this long-term project.

Step 1: Pick a topic.
Step 2: Research it.
Step 3: Design some way to make a difference in your topic area.
Step 4: Present to the class.

Keep in mind—even though you're kids now, you are the adults of tomorrow. You all can make a difference.

Sincerely,
Ms. Graham

HENRY

SCENE: *Table groups brainstorming social issues. Henry's group is celebrating because they missed Henry so much during the Whistler experiment.*

HENRY: Our team is back together again. I'm misty-eyed.

BLAKE: Yeah, I know. It was weird being split up for that Whistler thing.

HENRY: Fist bump! *(offering his hand)*

KAYLEY: *(not smiling)* Shut up. Let's get to work.

HENRY: Man, you're good. I got to work on my skills. *(hand still stretched out)*

BLAKE: *(fists-bumps Henry)*

KAYLEY: Let's do women's rights.

HENRY: We have to pick a current issue, not one from the past.

KAYLEY: Can you ever be serious?

HENRY: I AM being serious. Women can vote, right? They can have pretty much any job—fireman, policeman, soldier. . . .

AVIVA: Yeah, but listen to yourself. You just said "fire*man*" and "police*man*."

BLAKE: You want him to say fire*woman* and police*woman*?

AVIVA: I don't really care what he calls it—it shows that things are not totally equal.

KAYLEY: *(high-fives Aviva)* Plus all my dad's assistants are women. And all the bosses are men. What's that about?

BLAKE: Our principal's a woman. And our teacher's a woman.

HENRY: See—that's what I'm saying. What about global warming? Gun control? Animal rights? Bullying?

KAYLEY: There's a ton of issues that are important. But we have to pick one, right? And women's issues matter.

HENRY: People eat fried frog legs, you know. So . . . what about amphibian rights? How'd you like it if someone tried to fry up Kermit's legs?

MS. GRAHAM: *(leaning in)* I can't help overhearing. I have to agree with Kayley and Aviva that there are many current women's rights issues, both in this country and outside of it. Why don't you spend the rest of this period Googling some gender-equality issues on the computer? After you have more information, your team can decide.

HENRY: *(with sarcasm)* Frog-tastic.

SHARON

Every time Dad listens to the news
I hear about violence.
Shootings and terrorist attacks . . .
Awful things that make me
Want to cover my ears
And close my eyes.

Is that because awful things are happening all the time?
Or because violence makes exciting news?
And regular, peaceful stuff is too boring?
Either way, there's too much of it.

Kai suggests that
Our social issue be bullying
And all of a sudden, I realize that
The violence I hear about
Is really just grown-up bullying
In a different, more scary, form.

KAYLEY

Dear Ms. Graham,

Sometimes I'm glad I'll be at an all-girls school next year.
My mother thinks I'll get more personal attention and it will be
easier for me to focus without the Distraction of boys around.

I agree! I tell her that boys are always fidgeting and asking dumb questions the teacher already covered.

Ms. Graham, you suggested looking at other countries too. What about those places where young girls get forced into arranged marriages? This is a Great Topic—we're gonna rock this project and get an A plus plus plus!

Although there is one major problem: Blake Benson spends all his time drawing. He can hardly write—if he makes us get a B, my parents will have a fit. You don't want that, do you?

———

Dear Ms. Graham,

I'm all for group projects, but I think we should each be graded individually. Some of us work harder than others. Please consider this.

—Kayley

BLAKE

AVIVA

Date: October 30

During computer time I Googled the words "gender equality" and "gender inequality." So much information came up that I didn't know where to start. I made a list.

- Actresses make a ton of money when they're young, but when they get wrinkly and saggy they can't get good parts. Guy actors get paid a ton even when they're old. Look at Zac Efron. He still gets good parts and he's super-old.
- The US has had forty-five male presidents, and how many women presidents? ZERO? What is that about?
- US women aren't guaranteed paid time off from work after they have a baby. Out of 185 countries, the US is one of just three that doesn't guarantee this kind of paid time off. That's why Ima quit her job when I was born. Paying for day care or a babysitter cost almost as much money as she earned.

And then I found info from other countries that I can hardly believe:

- Like women not being able to pick who they marry.
- And women not having equal rights if they get divorced.
- Like not being allowed to dance in public.

- Like in some countries girls aren't allowed to go to school. Some sneak away to secret schools, but they're putting their lives at risk to do so.

Ms. Graham asked us what we'd do if we had a magic wand. End hunger and war, that's for sure. World peace. And I'd fix this thing with Emily. Tomorrow's Halloween, and this is the first year we won't be trick-or-treating together. Thinking about that gives me a sick feeling in my stomach, and I know the candy won't even taste good this year.

The other day I saw Emily's mom at the grocery store. She waved at me, all friendly, like she always did before, and I wanted to shrivel up to the size of a raisin. I thought she'd be angry with me for ditching her daughter. *I'm* angry with me.

CECILIA

Hola Abuelita,

Usually, I let my thoughts spin tornados in my mind, but I keep them inside my mouth. Today Kai asked me what topic I wanted to pick. This time my idea was right on the edge of my lips, and I let it spill out.

Poverty. People being homeless. I shared about how prima Maria, Mami, and I wrap Christmas gifts at the Sacred Heart Homeless Shelter in the city. We help deliver them, and every year I'm surprised at how many children and families live there. Even kids our age! Last year I talked to one of the little girls, and she said they'd lost their apartment when her mom had an accident and couldn't work for a few months. She was so sweet—I still think about her and wish I could've done more to help her. I hate that people have to live in poverty.

How many people live right on that edge, where one accident or a lost job can push them into homelessness? I asked Mami if that could ever happen to us. But she said because her prima Maria lives near, we'd help each other out.

Wow. I talked a lot. I probably said more in this conversation than I normally do in a week! Kai and Emily and Sharon looked at each other. And for the first time in my life, other kids chose *my* idea. It felt pretty awesome.

WORDS TO PRACTICE
poverty = *pobreza*
homeless = *sin hogar*
tornado = *tornado* (Don't you love it when words translate exactly? It's like a freebie.)

Besos y abrazos,
Cecilia

KAi

Hey, Frog!

I'm so glad we picked Cecilia's idea. She's so quiet it's easy to miss her, but today I noticed her eyes get sparkly when she talks.

Wait—I don't like girls yet.

Yes I do (a little).

Partly because I wanted to stop thinking about Cecilia, I brought Kermit to my table group today, and we blocked off a little area so he could jump around. When Cecilia was talking about the homeless shelter, I kept thinking about Blake Benson. He may not be in the same situation as the people Cecilia was talking about, but I'm guessing things aren't easy for him. We played some b-ball and skateboarded yesterday after school for two hours. He's pretty good—better than me, at least. He showed me how to ollie and grind, and I showed him my behind-the-back Rubik's Cube trick and gave him a stack of oatmeal raisin cookies.

Blake didn't say anything about home, but it was good times, you know? I think we'll do it again on Friday. And I asked him if he wanted to trick-or-treat with me. It's my tradition to dress up as a different Harry Potter character each year, even though I'm a little old for that. This year I'm going as Dumbledore, but I told Blake I have a Snape or Harry costume he can borrow. (Just in case he doesn't have one.)

CHAPTER 13

To my esteemed fifth-grade students,

Congratulations to each table group team! Last week, you all selected a social issue on which to focus.

Over the next few weeks, I encourage you to go a step further. Don't just study your topic; immerse yourself in it. Strive to understand it.

You will someday be running this world, and I challenge you to make it a better place. I can't wait to see what your creative minds come up with next.

Sincerely,
Ms. Graham

KAYLEY

Dear Ms. Graham,

What do you mean by "immerse ourselves" in our topic? We can't go swimming in it. *Sheesh!* We can't travel to places like Africa or Pakistan. I know Emily's dad does that kind of thing, but it's insane (!!!) if you ask me. I heard there were tarantulas the size of my hands in Africa. Eek!

You should tell us about Africa someday. My mother says you're from there. I don't know how, because you don't have an accent or anything. By the way, I was right about Blake Benson. He's the Worst Member of our team. Even Horrible Henry is better than Blake. He's the one who should be immersed, not us.

AVIVA

Date: November 14

Ms. Graham wants us to "immerse-ourselves-in-our-topics," so I *immersed* myself in my Google search. I brought Kermit out in his mini-carrier to join me.

The topic that interests me most is girls not being able to go to school. Here in America we all cry when summer is over and we have to go back to school. School feels like a "have to" instead of a "want to." But I bet if we couldn't go to school, we'd all be begging to go. I know I like regular school way better than homeschool.

So I clicked on the sites that focused on access to education. You won't *believe* what I found. There's a girl from Pakistan. Her name is Malala Yousafzai. Some members of a group called the Taliban climbed onto her bus and shot her in the face after she stood up for women's rights to be educated. Can you believe it?

She almost *died*. And now she's this advocate for women's access to education. She won the Nobel Peace Prize and helped to open a school for Syrian refugees, all when she was just a teenager. Uber-ly cool.

Malala is the opposite of me. She speaks her mind, and her danger is real. What's my danger? That someone will judge me? Or misunderstand me? Or be mad at me? I did write that anonymous note when Ms. Graham played that awful Whistler game, but I did it secretly, so it's not the same.

I am making a promise to myself. I will try to speak up more. If Malala can do it, *so can I.*

PS Kayley's getting stress-y again, like she did with the Egg-Off. That girl does everything loudly, and I think it's contagious, because I now feel like a stress case too. Maybe I should write her a sticky note that says "Chill."

SHARON

Every Thursday night
My church
Hosts a soup kitchen
For families who are struggling.
But they don't just make soup,
There's bread and salad,
And something else hot . . . usually pasta.

Plus it's nearly Thanksgiving,

So maybe there'll be pumpkin pie?

My grandma volunteers there twice a month.

Maybe she can bring my whole social-issues team

So we can "immerse ourselves."

If Grandma drives us,

It'll be kind of like I'm hosting.

I don't do that kind of thing very often,

But I did have Emily over last week

And I have to say

It was really nice.

EMILY

Status: 😊

Dear Hope,

Mom gave a thumbs-up to the soup kitchen field trip. Normally churches give me this weird "you don't belong," "you don't get it" kind of feeling. Maybe because we've never gone as a family? I went a couple of times with Kayley's parents, but I always felt like I was wearing pants that didn't fit. Just uncomfortable and fidgety. I didn't get the prayers. I didn't get the songs. And the books smelled funny. Sometimes I wish Mom went to church, or Dad even, so I'd understand this stuff.

But when we helped in the soup kitchen at Sharon's church,

it was a whole different thing. It was all about the working. Sharon and I got to wear plastic gloves, and we arranged the bread in a basket. We made patterns with it so it looked really nice (brown roll, white roll, brown roll, white roll . . . like that). They didn't let us kids actually serve the soup. Probably because they were afraid we'd spill it or burn ourselves. But we got to hand out cups of water and talk to people, and that was cool.

I wish Mom had come with us. But she didn't feel up to it. Again.

Love and luck,
Emily

SHARON

My grandma
Has crinkly wrinkles and gray hair,
Like every other grandma in the world,
But there's something about the bounce to her step,
The dangly earrings,
And the hair that hangs to her shoulder blades
That makes her seem young.

She tells me she's a hippie
Who never grew up.

She smells like sugar and iced tea
And her skin is so soft it feels like a baby's.

She let me sit in the front seat (Mom never does that)
So we could fit my teammates in her red Honda
And she gave up all control over the music choice.
I love Grandma.
We car-danced all the way there . . .
And all the way back.

CECiLiA

Hola Abuelita,

I can't wait to tell you about our soup kitchen project. ¡Guau! Sharon's abuelita makes my heart sing. You wouldn't believe her—she doesn't seem like a grandmother at all, more like a cool tía, and I can't see her age anywhere except for her face. She drove so fast I had to grip my seat so that I didn't tip. She tapped her fingers on the wheel to the beat of the music, like she was dancing and driving at the same time. She knew everyone at the church, and she gave out hugs like dulces.

The soup needed more spices, but no one seemed to notice. The people filled their bowls and plates and ate quietly. Kai stood next to me, serving salad and making me laugh. I'm not used to so much attention. It's nice, I guess.

When I left, Sharon's abuelita kissed me on the cheek, and

that made me want to cry. I miss you SO MUCH, Abuelita! FaceTiming is not the same as having you in person. When I'm a grown-up and I can travel by myself, I'll visit you every summer. Can't wait until I'm eighteen!

WORDS TO PRACTICE
spices = *especias*

Besos y abrazos,
Cecilia

HENRY

SCENE: *Classroom work groups, Henry wondering if it's possible to die from boredom.*

MS. GRAHAM: *(hovers)* How's your research on women's access to education going?

KAYLEY: Slow. *(glares at Henry and Blake)* Seems like the WOMEN are the only ones working here.

MS. GRAHAM: *(pulls up a chair to sit down)* Have any of your grandparents told you stories about walking ten miles in the snow to school?

HENRY: Barefoot, right? That's like one of those old-school stories parents tell their kids to make them behave. Just like the "eat your veggies, there are starving kids in Africa" bit.

MS. GRAHAM: Well. *(quiet for a moment)* The truth is that there *are* hungry children in much of the world. And those aren't just stories. Even in America, a good education used to be harder to get. Some kids who lived on farms had to miss school during seasons when there was work to be done on the farm. Children really did walk miles to get to school each day. Can you all think of other examples?

AVIVA: How people fought so hard to end segregation in schools?

MS. GRAHAM: *(smiles)* Yes. Good example, Aviva. And as you know from your research, in other countries, sometimes education for women is forbidden or just not accessible. I was born in a part of West Africa called Sierra Leone, and there weren't enough schools and teachers to educate everyone.

BLAKE: Does that mean some of the kids don't get to go to school at all, even if they want to?

MS. GRAHAM: That's exactly right.

HENRY: *(surprised because he had NO CLUE that Ms. Graham was from Africa, and thinks this is fantastically cool)*

KAYLEY: Did you go to school in Sierra Leone, Ms. Graham? I've been wondering.

MS. GRAHAM: I did not. I was adopted by an American family and brought here when I was three. It was a time of civil war in my country. *(stands up)* I did go back and teach in Sierra Leone the first few years after I earned my graduate degree.

Bell rings for recess. Twenty-two minutes of Freedom!!! Kids grab snacks from backpacks and make a mad dash outside.

HENRY: I curse this research on women's access to education. Does Mrs. Graham have to enlighten us all the time? Now I feel guilty if I fake a stomachache to get out of class!

BLAKE: Poor baby.

HENRY: You see, Kayley? That's how it's done.

KAYLEY: *(face red)* I'm tired of you guys fooling around all class. Henry, at least you do part of the work, but Blake—you do NOTHING. All you ever do is draw. This is a group project and we get a group grade. If we get a B or a C, it will be all your fault. What's your problem?

BLAKE: *(face getting splotchy, turning and storming toward soccer field)*

KAYLEY: I'm trying to talk to you. *(grabs at his shirt, yanking him backward)* I'm not going to let a DUMMY pull my grade down. How DUMB are you, exactly?

BLAKE: *(turns to Kayley and shoves her, hard)*

KAYLEY: *(lands on her butt in mud)*

BLAKE: *(wipes at his eyes)*

HENRY: You're a jerk, Kayley Barrette. I don't care how smart or rich or pretty you are. You need to get a grip. *(leads Blake away, and leaves Kayley in the mud)*

KAYLEY

Dear Ms. Graham,

I let that Blake Benson have it today at recess. Big-time. I didn't mean to get all in his face like that, but he just kept right on walking, practically running. I grabbed for his shirt, and then I said something mean. It slipped out, like soap between my fingers.

Then Blake whirled around and shoved me. *Hard.* I flew back and landed on my butt. I had to go to the nurse's office and borrow a pair of loaner jeans because my butt was all covered with Yuck.

Principal Severns asked me what happened, but I didn't tell. Because Blake was crying. He got those hiccupy breaths and he couldn't even talk. That's why I didn't tell.

Ms. Graham, the good thing is that you can't get mad at me, since you're not supposed to be reading these journal entries. Besides, you can't expect me to sit here, day after day, with such irritating seatmates and never speak up for myself. I'm sorry I said something mean, but nobody's perfect. I'm allowed to make mistakes too, you know.

Question: If I'm the one with a ruined pair of pants, why is it I'm still feeling so bad?

BLAKE   WICKED WITCH OF THE WEST

CHAPTER 14

CECILIA

Hola Abuelita,

We talked about education in school today, because one of the table groups is studying "access to education." I'm glad they're researching that topic, because, hello?—do you guys even realize how lucky we are?

Education is like gold to people who want it, but I think the people who have it forget how valuable it is. Like, for example, Mami risked her life to travel to the United States so that I could be born in this country and be able to go to public school here.

Sometimes I get frustrated with the other kids. Like today, Blake pushed Kayley. It's not okay to strike someone else no matter how irritating they are, but I heard what she said, and it made my mouth drop to the floor! Nobody is talking about what happened. Blake didn't tell on Kayley (no surprise), and Kayley didn't tell on Blake (big surprise)!

Kayley has a huge blind spot. She only sees the world through her own eyes. She doesn't realize there are so many other ways to live. Someone needs to put a sticky note on her desk that says, "Open Your Eyes."

surprise = *sorpresa*

> Besos y abrazos,
> Cecilia

———

Dear Ms. Graham,

I don't think you're being fair with this social-issues project. Every single day I have to sit in class, irritated because I have two group members who goof off. That's half my group! I'm not just a little irritated. I'm a LOT irritated.

The other reason is that these are big problems—it's not like we can do anything that Matters for this project. So what's the Point?

> —Kayley

———

Dear Kayley,

Thank you for raising this concern. If you are feeling frustrated, I imagine others are as well. I will speak to the class today.

> Sincerely,
> Ms. Graham

HENRY

SCENE: *Ms. Graham tries to convince the students that this assignment has a purpose. Typical.*

MS. GRAHAM: It's come to my attention that some students are feeling discouraged about the social-issues project. Let's discuss this.

CLASS: *(quiet)*

KAYLEY: It does seem sort of pointless.

MS. GRAHAM: How so?

BLAKE: Well, there's all these sad things happening in the world. And it's not like we can actually do anything about it.

MS. GRAHAM: Has anyone ever heard of the butterfly effect?

AVIVA: How a caterpillar transforms into a butterfly? Is it the idea that people can change?

MS. GRAHAM: I really like that, Aviva. I love that human beings have the capacity for change. This particular term refers to something different, though.

KAI: Isn't it that when a butterfly flaps its wings, it might change something across the world? Like some kind of ripple or something?

MS. GRAHAM: Yes! It's the idea that a small change in one thing can lead to big changes in other things. Like for example, I know one of our teams served food at a soup kitchen. Imagine a hungry man who came to eat there—let's say his name is Fred.

Pretend Fred came to the soup kitchen so hungry that he could hardly think. He left with a full stomach. And because he was full, he had enough energy to apply for a job. What might happen next?

KAI: Maybe Fred's a hard worker and they like him.

HENRY: Maybe Fred gets promoted. Or gets a better job.

AVIVA: Maybe he doesn't have to worry about being hungry anymore.

MS. GRAHAM: Let's say all these things are true. He saves his money, and after many years of hard work and investment, Fred winds up wealthy, and he credits his life to that one meal at the soup kitchen. Let's say he wants to give back. What might he do?

SHARON: Open up his own soup kitchen!

EMILY: Adopt a bunch of kids.

BLAKE: Build a huge frog habitat.

MS. GRAHAM: Right! He could do a wide variety of things to help others. That one meal, that one kind act, could snowball into a thousand kind acts and then could affect many lives. That's the butterfly effect.

SHARON: That's cool!

HENRY: Can the same be said for something negative? Like if, for example, someone is mean to someone else? *(looks at Kayley pointedly)*

MS. GRAHAM: Absolutely. Anything and everything we do—positive or negative, big or small—can influence other people and the world.

KAI: Is it like what we did for Kermit? We rescued him. He'd have died if he was left outside. But we saved his life.

HENRY: Yes, and he somehow *(looks at Blake)* hopped his way in here to our class. We're frog heroes. Making a difference, one frog at a time.

KAYLEY: So we saved a frog. Big deal.

HENRY: Maybe because we saved Kermit, one of us will go on to be a famous biologist who solves global warming and saves our planet. It's the frog effect.

MS. GRAHAM: Yes! Remember, change can take place on multiple levels. Even change within yourself is change.

HENRY: *(whispers)* Maybe some of us will set personal goals. Like maybe to not call people mean names?

KAYLEY: *(red face)*

MS. GRAHAM: Refocus on your social-issues project. Think about whether there's something you can actually *do* to make a difference. Remember, even something small can have a big impact. Document your efforts in your journals. I challenge you all.

HENRY: Ooh. A challenge. Me likes that.

EMILY

Status: 😶

Dear Hope,

Ms. Graham has me thinking. How can we truly "immerse" ourselves in our social issue if we're sleeping in our comfy beds every night?

We're supposed to "challenge ourselves." Does organizing bread rolls at a soup kitchen somehow make me understand what it's like to be poor? Sharon and I talked about this at lunch today. I told her that my dad would say no, that we still have no clue what it's like to be poor.

Then I told her all about his work as an investigative reporter. One time he spent a week in a refugee camp just so he could write about the experience. Sharon is SO interested in my dad's work. It makes me remember how supremely cool it is.

I think I'll get to Skype with him this week. I hope so. Maybe he'll have some ideas? Hmmm. My wheels are turning. . . .

Love and luck,
Emily

SHARON

I am untethered.
A lonely ship on the sea
With high-powered speed
And nowhere to go.

But now I spy a direction.
A purpose.
I want to do something *real*.
To understand what it's truly like
To be homeless.
Maybe then I can find a way
To make a difference,
Just like Emily's dad.

Ms. Graham says,
"Immerse yourself."
How about being homeless for a night?
That's diving in the pool at the deep end
and swimming all the way down
until our ears feel like
they'll burst from the pressure.
Full immersion.

CHAPTER 15

BLAKE

AVIVA

Date: November 30

Dear Malala,

You don't know me. I am an American girl. I think you are SO brave. We are studying social issues in school, and I would like to learn more about how to make it safe for girls around the world to get an education. I saw your book in the library and I'm checking it out. Can't wait to read it.

Sincerely,
Aviva Levy

———

I'm trying to channel Malala whenever I can. She didn't let anything stop her.

But me—I still can't get up my nerve to ask Emily to walk to school again (even though we wrote letters, it's too weird to ask her). Since I'm still afraid to walk alone—it's easier to keep biking.

But Malala can be my inspiration for our school project. Ms. Graham said even something small can make a difference. Maybe we can offer after-school tutoring for the lower-grade kids?

KAI

Dear Frog,

Sharon says she wants us to do more to "immerse ourselves." We went to the soup kitchen, so I say we've already put the butterfly effect into action. Right?

But there's no convincing that girl. She's calling a lunchtime meeting. She said it's Urgent! I feel kind of weird sitting with girls at lunch. Maybe I'll just stand.

I overheard Kayley's group talking about how women get paid less than men. That bothers me. If my social-issues group is a good example, girls work *way* hard. And Mom works way hard for sure. She hardly ever sits still. Even on Sundays when we watch our family movie and we all squish onto the couch together, Mom lugs the ironing board down to the living room so she can iron while we watch. Maybe next Sunday I'll help her.

EMILY

Status: 😬
Dear Hope,

Sharon invited Cecilia and Kai to sit with us for lunch. Kai just stood there all fidgety. Like he was only planning on staying a minute. Sharon passed around a bag of pita chips. And then she laid out her plan (which she said was inspired by our conversation about my dad).

The PLAN: We could all spend the night in a homeless shelter. We'd bring our journals and take notes, and this would help us figure out what homeless people actually need and what we could do to make a difference. Our parents wouldn't have to know. We'd tell them we were sleeping over at each other's houses. We'd be together, so we'd be safe. And then we could show Ms. Graham (and the whole class) how we "challenged ourselves."

Ooh! I could write about this. My first experience with true in-the-trenches journalism. Maybe if I write something EXTRAORDINARY, Dad will help me polish it? Maybe Mom will be proud and it'll pull her out of her sadness? She's lonely (me too). Only . . . doesn't she see that I'm right here? She has me for company, if she wants it.

Cecilia suggested a vote.

I'm in.

Love and luck,
Emily

CECiLiA

Hola Abuelita,

Sharon's idea makes my heart shake. Taking a bus all the way to the city? By ourselves? Sleeping at Sacred Heart shelter for a whole night? It was fine to visit with Mami, but to stay there overnight? I don't know. That idea kind of freaks me out.

160

I reminded the group that Ms. Graham said "something small" can still make a difference. I thought maybe we could just do a bake sale and donate the money. I suggested we take a vote. I was pretty sure Emily and Kai would vote for the bake sale. Only one by one, everyone voted for the trip to Sacred Heart. So . . . I did too.

Sharon says our parents won't understand. I know one thing for sure: If I ask Mami, she'll say no. Sharon's right that if I want to go, I can't ask. But . . . this feels wrong. Abuelita, I wish you were here to give me consejos. I definitely need your wisdom.

<u>WORDS TO PRACTICE</u>
shelter = *albergue*

Besos y abrazos,
Cecilia

KAYLEY

Dear Ms. Graham,

It's Unfair to ask Blake Benson to do a project like this. It's Unfair to our team and it's unfair to him. I know I called him a DUMMY but I don't really think he is. He's smart about some things, like math and science and art and sports—anything without a lot of reading and writing, but more thinking and doing. We all know Blake gets pulled out of class for Resource Class, but maybe it's not working.

161

What kind of education is Blake getting if all he's doing is drawing and wasting class time? What if we change the topic from "Women's Access to Education" and just think about "Access to Education"?

Ooh! I think I'm onto something here. My mother's always got one Project or another. Now I have one, too—Blake Benson. Only this has to be a secret mission. If Blake knows that he's my project, he'll fight it. I doubt there's extra credit for being nice, but I'm not sure if I care.

Update: I tried out my plan today. I asked Blake Benson to find video clips on "Access to Education." And then I told him that when we get to the presentation part, he can design the art on our poster. Maybe reading and writing aren't his thing, but drawing sure is. This way at least he's doing *something*, instead of sitting around and laughing at every irritating thing Henry says.

Today he really worked for the first time. It was pretty cool, seeing him get into the project. He hardly made eye contact with me, though, probably because of the DUMMY thing. He'll get over it. I guess it was nice of Blake not to tell on me. Of course, I didn't tell on him either, but still.

EMILY

Status: 😔
Dear Hope,

I'm feeling guilty already. I'm not naturally a sneaky kid. I'm the opposite. I can't even sneak snacks into a movie theater.

But tonight I lied and told Mom I'd be spending Saturday night with Aviva. She doesn't know we're not friends anymore. I'm always trying to cheer Mom up, so I haven't shared any of the school drama. I used to tell her every time someone at school so much as sneezed.

Speaking of sneezing, Aviva's animals make the back of my throat itch something awful. When I told Mom I'd be at Aviva's, she just said, "Great." Then she told me to remember to bring my allergy meds. I grabbed my journal so I could document everything, and tried to ignore the guilt.

> Love and luck (now I'll really need
> luck so I don't get caught!),
> Emily

CECiLiA

Hola Abuelita,

I'm not going to send you this letter. I don't want to disappoint you—if you read this, you'd read it with shame! You know I never lie to Mami. I mean, sure, we argue sometimes. But . . . we do have trust between us. Today I'm breaking it.

I told Mami that I'm sleeping over at a friend's house to work on a school project. This is a trick (and why I feel terrible)—because I know Mami would do anything for my education. She'd get another job and donate all the money to my school if she didn't need to sleep. Seriously. That's how much she loves it.

I know lying is wrong, but isn't sometimes doing the wrong thing for the right reason okay? Still . . . I can't even bear to imagine you reading this, Abuelita. I'll have to rip this section out.

Besos y abrazos,
Cecilia

EMILY

Status: 😐

Dear Hope,

I'm writing to you on the bus. I have never in my entire life ridden on a city bus without a parent. My stomach is churning with that sick-guilty feeling for lying to Mom. She didn't ask me one single question. Is it because she trusts me so completely? (Okay, that makes me feel horrible.)

I promise I won't do anything like this again. I know it's for a good cause, but my heart is all fluttery. Just like that time I thought it was a good idea to roller-skate down Kayley's steep driveway. It looked like fun, but I forgot about those tiny pebbles that can get caught up in a roller skate wheel. I went for it anyway, and I have the scars to prove it.

My mind's tangled up with worries and excitement, and I'm thinking maybe this wasn't such a great idea.

Love and luck,
Emily

CHAPTER 16

AVIVA

Date: December 9

I gotta write this down! Thank *goodness* I brought my journal home this weekend, because I feel like I swallowed a horse bit, and the sharp metal part is shredding my insides.

I *lied*! Ten minutes ago. A big old *whopping* lie. Mrs. Thompson (Emily's mom) dropped by. I figured she was here to tell Ima what a rotten person I've been, but no, she said Emily forgot her green allergy pills for tonight's sleepover. *Uh . . . what?*

I got all confused for a second, but then I figured Emily must've told her mom she was sleeping here. And the least I could do was protect her so she wouldn't get in trouble. So instead of saying I hadn't invited Emily at all, I just said she hadn't come *yet*. (Half-lie? Half-truth?)

Mrs. Thompson stared at me for the longest moment ever, and then she started walking in circles, saying that Emily left her house hours ago and oh-my-g-d-where-could-she-be? Her voice got louder and louder. Ima came running downstairs to see what was the matter, and they both started panicking, and I couldn't handle all the grown-up freak-outs (which are *terrifying*), plus they weren't paying attention to me, so I escaped up to my room.

Writing in my journal is helping me think this through. Because Emily wasn't planning to come in the first place, right? Maybe she wanted to go to the movies by herself without her mom knowing. What if she met some boy on the internet, which they always tell us not to do? What if she's being held hostage somewhere? *Oh no. What if someone hurts her?* Why didn't she give me a heads-up? At least then I could've talked her out of anything stupid. Or if she's just being sneaky, I'd have known how to cover for her.

Ohhh. Yeah. A sad thought sinks in. Maybe she *did* want to talk to me but was afraid because of the way I've been acting. Maybe that's why. She didn't think she *could* talk to me. Just like I didn't talk to her about Tattoo Man. Just the thought of him sucks the breath out of me. *Oh. My. G-d.* Maybe he really was a kidnapper? What if he kidnapped Emily? I should've told someone. If Emily is kidnapped it will be *all my fault!*

I need to talk to someone! My mom? No—I'll get in trouble for not telling earlier. I'll call Kayley. My heart is Ping-Ponging around in my chest and now I'm crying and I don't think I'm thinking straight but I know I have to do something and I just want Emily to be okay.

KAYLEY

Dear Ms. Graham,

Aviva just called me, all hysterical. I could hardly understand her, she was crying so hard. So I made her take deep breaths and start over.

There's a Kidnapper on the loose! I can't believe Aviva was almost kidnapped and she didn't tell anyone! *What's her problem?* Who knows why Emily said she was going to Aviva's when she wasn't, but I told Aviva she needs to tell the truth right away. Who cares if Emily gets mad? She'll get over it.

Plus I told Aviva *I'll* tell if *she* doesn't. This is a big deal. After I got off the phone I ran downstairs to tell my mother and she got stress-y right away. She parked me in front of the television and told me to keep the doors to the house locked and stay inside. Then she left, I guess to go over to Aviva's and help them figure this mess out.

I have an idea. I'll call all the people on Emily's team. We have a class contact list that the Room Mom puts together in September every year. Maybe Emily's at one of their houses and her mom got confused about where she was going?

PS Weird. I can't get ahold of anyone from Emily's team. No one answered at Sharon's house. I couldn't try Cecilia because there's no number for her on our class contact list. At Kai's house I talked to this little kid who kept saying, "Hi. I Jayla." She couldn't have been more than three. I kept asking her to get Kai on the phone and she said, "I not Kai. I Jayla."

PPS I hope Emily is okay. Now I feel a tiny bit bad about my meat sauce joke.

PPPS I'm FREAKING out! I can't be here ALONE. What if the Kidnapper comes here? My mother told me not to leave the house, but she didn't tell me I couldn't have anyone over.

HENRY

SCENE: *Phone call between Kayley and Henry. When phone rings, Henry is vegging on his bed.*

HENRY: *(answers phone)* Hello?

KAYLEY: Hi. It's Kayley the Jerk.

HENRY: *(sits up)* Apology accepted.

KAYLEY: That wasn't an apology. It was me trying to be funny.

HENRY: Oh, I get it. Hey—that is funny!

KAYLEY: Enough small talk. Something serious is going on and I need your help. Can you get over to my house?

HENRY: How serious?

KAYLEY: Life-and-death serious.

HENRY: I'm there.

BLAKE

AVIVA

Date: December 9

I knew I had to confess once Kayley called me to say that her mom was on her way over. So I crept back downstairs, where Ima was still trying to calm Mrs. Thompson down. She'd made her a cup of hot tea and was helping her think things through . . . asking if maybe Emily's dad was in town, or if maybe Emily could have made a stop on the way to my house? Ima shot me a look too, and I knew that was because she didn't know Emily was coming over. I'd done that before, invited Emily without checking with Ima. But this time I hadn't invited her at all!

This seemed like a good place for me to confess, so in a teeny-tiny, about-to-cry voice, I told Mrs. Thompson that Emily and I didn't *actually* have plans today. Her face turned so red that I worried she wasn't getting enough oxygen. Ima jumped in and said maybe Mrs. Thompson misheard Emily, maybe she was spending the night at another friend's. This seemed to calm Mrs. Thompson a bit. But then Kayley's mother got here and started grilling me about Tattoo Man, and the questions kept flying at me from all directions, and I burst into tears.

We called everyone from our class to try to track Emily down. Funny, we got ahold of everyone except for five people. And three of them were Emily's teammates. Kai's mom said he went camping with a friend from Boy Scouts. Cecilia doesn't seem to have a phone. Sharon's mom said she was staying with a cousin but then called back ten minutes later, wondering if

Sharon and Emily might be together. Apparently, Sharon wasn't where she was supposed to be either.

Could the whole table group be together?

HENRY

SCENE: *Kayley's place, eating soft cheese and kiwi, trying to figure out where Emily might have gone.*

HENRY: Your snacks are almost as weird as mine.

KAYLEY: Yeah. I know. Chips are forbidden in my house.

HENRY: The agony! A house without shrimp chips.

BLAKE: Say what? Shrimp chips?

HENRY: Yep. Some of my snacks are deceiving. You can't tell what they're made of just by looking at them. Upon first glance, they appear to be run-of-the-mill packaged foods, but they've got a fishy twist. Shrimp-flavored chips, jerky made of cuttlefish . . . instead of meatballs, we've got fish balls. You get the gist.

KAYLEY: Maybe I should bring out the caviar.

HENRY: If this wasn't such a rotten situation, I'd tell you that's funny.

KAYLEY: If this wasn't such a rotten situation, I'd tell you thank you.

BLAKE: *(drinks a seltzer with a beet-red face)*

KAYLEY: Blake, how far did you walk to get here? Your face looks like a tomato.

BLAKE: Far.

KAYLEY: I'll have my mother drive you both home when we're done.

HENRY: Sure.

BLAKE: No thanks. I'm okay.

HENRY: I think that's the Jerk's way of saying she's sorry that she's such a jerk.

KAYLEY: Hey!

BLAKE

EMILY

Status: 😟

Dear Hope,

Change of plans.

We left Sacred Heart. The shelter line snaked around the building and down the street. After a while, people started walking away, grumbling that it was full and how dare it be full, and where was the government funding, and there better be good spots left under the bridge.

Kai said, "They don't have enough room. Should we call it off?"

Sharon dropped her sleeping bag to the ground. "We could." She looked like she wanted to say something else but wasn't sure how. "I guess we already know one thing homeless people need—and that's more room at the shelter. Or maybe more shelters?"

But it's not like any of us can build a new shelter.

So then Sharon said maybe we should check out that place under the bridge. "Just to see if we can learn more about what they need. There might be something we can actually help with. This is our chance to do something real. We can't give up now, can we?"

I guess not.

Love and luck,
Emily

PS Kai keeps looking at Cecilia. I might be wrong, but I think he *likes* her likes her.

PPS Nobody knows this, but I brought a knife. A super-sharp one Mom uses to slice vegetables. I've got it wrapped up in a towel in my backpack.

KAi

Hey, Frog!

This is intense. We're all hunkered down under a bridge. Cecilia keeps fiddling with the cross around her neck, and I wonder if she's nervous. My feet are freezing.

So no joke—it's pretty creepy down here.

Like, really creepy.

I'm the only guy in our group. In books and movies the guys always protect the girls and I think that's what I'm supposed to do now, but this is serious stuff. We're alone in the dark in the city under a bridge.

My radar's going off.

Like time to jam. Let's get moving.

I always hear Mom tell my big brother, Thomas, that if he gets stuck somewhere, he should call. No matter how late, and no matter why. That we take no chances. We can't climb in other people's brains and know what they're thinking; we've got to be smarter than the situations we're placed in. If I can get my hands on a phone, maybe I can call Mom? She'd pick us up. Or call Thomas? He'd know what to do.

SHARON

I'm freezing.
I never before realized
How much I like to be warm.
And clean.
Clean clothes. Clean bed.
Clean skin. Clean hair.
Nothing about the bridge is clean.
I feel dirty and itchy from the moment we arrive.
Maybe it's the way
Eyes stick to us
Like flies on flypaper.

All of a sudden I realize
This is the kind of thing my mom would call
A Bad Idea.
The kind of thing parents warn us about
And protect us from.
But our parents can't protect us now.
They don't even know we're here.
No one knows we're here.

CHAPTER 17

CECILIA

Hola Abuelita,

I didn't want to come in the first place! That's why I suggested the vote. Why didn't my feet listen to my brain? And I'm so cold. My toes and fingertips are the worst.

Now I think everyone else is realizing the same thing. I can tell by the way Emily's biting her nails, Sharon's eyes are wide, and Kai's edging closer and closer to us. There's a man who keeps looking at us. He's got long stringy hair and tattoos everywhere. Now he's talking to some other grungy men. He's pointing at us and shaking his head. Why is he watching us? What is he saying about us?

I've got that want-to-cry feeling, where my throat is tight and my nose aches. I'm not sure I can hold it back. I reach for Emily's hand and try to remind myself that I'm not alone.

WORDS TO PRACTICE
No words today. You'll never see this letter.

Besos y abrazos,
Cecilia

KAI

Hey, Frog!

It's so cold my bones hurt and the tip of my nose feels like it might chip off like a piece of ice. The girls are scared, I can tell—even Sharon, and I've never seen her scared before.

I just wish that man would stop looking at us.

I've got to do something.

We've got to go. NOW.

AVIVA

Date: December 9

Dear G-d,

If Emily's okay, I promise *never* to complain about chores.

If she's okay, I'll confess to her the truth about the cheese pizza.

If she's okay, I'll be a better friend, I promise.

Please!

KAYLEY

Dear Ms. Graham,

Things are pretty Bad. No one knows where Emily is. My mother came to pick me up, and Blake and Henry too. Now we're all sitting in Aviva's living room, trying to eat Greek pizza. The feta and spinach are making me want to hurl, because I can't stop thinking about how I told Emily there was meat in the school pizza sauce. And now she might be kidnapped for real.

The cops are trying to track down Emily, Kai, Sharon, and Cecilia. They think maybe they're all together, especially since it looks like Emily lied to her mom in the first place tonight. I know I haven't spent much time with Emily this school year, but I have known her since kindergarten. She's never been a liar before.

AViVA

Date: December 9

This is *all my fault*. I should have told about Tattoo Man right away. Ima gave me a big old lecture and started crying, because I'd been asking her to drive me to school and she'd been saying no, but of course if she'd known she'd have dropped-everything-to-take-me.

And don't I know how-important-safety-is, and haven't I been listening to them, and all-that-fuss about private school when this is exactly why I need one, because I'm clearly incapable of making safe decisions. She got *really* mad then, and shook her finger in my face, and yelled about me not speaking up.

I think I shrank to nothingness right there on the spot. And then I cried so hard my brain felt like it might explode.

Kayley put her arm around me, all protective, and she smelled like bubble gum, and asked me to come with her to drop Blake and Henry at home. I said yes because I didn't want Ima to keep yelling at me.

At first Ima said I was grounded and couldn't go with Kayley. But then she changed her mind, saying she should keep Emily's mom company until there was some news. Kayley's mother promised she'd watch us like hawks.

Kayley called shotgun, so I sat squished in the backseat between the two boys until we dropped Blake off. I had that hiccupy crying that doesn't stop and I felt *awful*.

HENRY

Today felt like a movie. I couldn't get any of this down until I got home tonight. My brain is still Hula-Hooping around inside my skull—it was THAT kind of day.

$$$

SCENE: *Squashed in the back of a red Corvette. Written by the up-and-coming director Henry (who will someday make millions so that he can buy ten Corvettes).*

KAYLEY: Aviva, stop crying. It's going to be okay.

AVIVA: *(sniffles)*

KAYLEY: Seriously. They're probably all together. They probably snuck off to a movie or something. It's the most logical explanation.

AVIVA: *(sniffles)*

KAYLEY: Stop crying! Can someone distract her or something? Henry, what good are your jokes if you can't whip them out at the right time?

HENRY: Oh. So I was thinking this was a bad time for jokes.

KAYLEY: It's a horrible time for jokes, but tell one anyway.

HENRY: Oh good, because I've been dying to say this but I thought it would be bad timing. So Mrs. Barrette, about this car . . . I'm turning sixteen in less than six years. By that time, this Corvette will be a shabby old thing. It'd make a great birthday present. Hint-hint.

KAYLEY: *(sarcastic)* Very funny.

HENRY: What? You told me to. Plus this is a once-in-a-lifetime opportunity for me. You can't blame me for trying.

BLAKE: Uh . . . you can just drop me here at the park.

MRS. BARRETTE: Blake—there's a child missing out there. No way! I'm walking you right to your front door.

BLAKE: Uh. It's the next left. Number 872.

KAYLEY: Maybe we can walk him up?

MRS. BARRETTE: *(pulls over)* If you all go together, that's fine.

HENRY: *(climbs out of car)* Now we can stalk you, Blake. We know where you live.

AVIVA: *(trying to talk while crying)* Henry—today—is not—a good day—for that kind—of joke.

HENRY: Oops. Sorry. My bad.

BLAKE: *(leads group around the side to garage door, looks uncomfortable)* Thanks, guys. Aviva, don't worry. They'll find her.

KAYLEY: We have to wait until you get in. Mother's orders.

BLAKE: *(unlocks door, then opens it a crack to slip in)*

KAYLEY: *(pushes door open, revealing that the garage has been converted into an apartment)*

EVERYONE: *(silent)*

BLAKE: This is just for a little while. We're getting another place soon.

KAYLEY: No—it's cute. You all did a great job fixing it up. It looks like a college dorm.

KITTEN: Meow.

BLAKE: *(scoops up kitten)* This is my newest roommate. She keeps me company.

HENRY: *(backs up)* Achoo! I'm allergic to cats. That's my cue to leave.

KAYLEY: Funny coincidence. I'm allergic too. Only I'm allergic to YOU!

HENRY: *(talks to Blake while backing up out of the room)* Is it just me, or is she getting funnier? *Achoo!*

KAYLEY

Dear Ms. Graham,

I was so curious about why Blake kept trying to get my mother to drop him off somewhere else. That's why I volunteered to walk him up. Of course I had no idea that he lives in a GARAGE!!!!! Like the place you park extra cars. I have never heard of something like this in my whole life. Doesn't it get cold? Is it even safe? Did you know this, Ms. Graham?

They have it set up pretty nice, but it's still a garage! What happens if he has to pee at night? Does he go in the regular house? Or in the bushes outside? Or walk down to the convenience store? And what about showers? I'm way too polite to ask any of those questions.

I know I am going to remember this night Forever. Only I really hope I remember it because it was a great big adventure and we find Emily and she's okay . . . not because . . . of something terrible.

CHAPTER 18

KAi

Dear Frog,

We're all sitting in a square room. We are not free to leave. Yeah. I just said that. Every time I think about what Mom and Dad are going to say when they get this call . . . I want to disappear.

I'm writing in my journal, trying not to *stress*. Let me tell you what happened. So back at the bridge, I got the girls to agree this was a BAD idea, and we needed to GO. We packed up real quick and started walking back to the shelter. Sharon dug in the bottom of her backpack to pull out a cell phone. I screeched, "Cell phone? You had a cell phone this whole time?"

And she snapped, "I'm not stupid enough to pull it out in front of everyone. It'd get stolen!" Then she started looking for a taxi service. We had less than ten dollars even if we pooled our money together, but Sharon promised her grandma would pay for the cab . . . if we took one to her house. Sharon said, "I got us into this mess, and I'll get us out!"

But then all of a sudden, that creepy dude with tattoos blocked our path. "Where're you going?" and "You gotta stay here!"

Emily and Cecilia turned on the tears right away, and Sharon stood real tall like you would if you came face-to-face with a bear in the woods. She told him to STAY AWAY from us in this booming-loud voice. I stood tall too, and stepped in front of the girls. I tried to think fast but I felt scrambled, all the advice my parents have given me over the years playing in my head.

But then Emily pulled out this knife. And it was a KNIFE. Like this huge gleaming blade that looked like it could gut the guy in seconds, and that did the trick. He backed up two steps and kept saying, "Stay here, kids. You gotta stay here."

All of a sudden these bright lights blinded us and it was the cops. And I thought, "Here we go. What're the police gonna think we're doing down here? And with Emily holding a *knife*?" I remembered the talk my parents gave me about snap judgments. I kept totally quiet and still and made sure to keep my hands in clear sight at all times. The cops made Emily drop the knife and Cecilia was wailing like someone died and we had to stay super-still until they decided we weren't criminals and wrapped us in blankets and sat us down to talk.

I guess that dude with the tattoos called the cops himself. He recognized us from our neighborhood, and he was worried about us being in such a dangerous place by ourselves. He wasn't a bad guy after all, just an ex-soldier who'd been living out of his car with his dog for a while. I guess we assumed what kind of guy he is based on how he looked.

I can still hardly catch my breath, and my brain is spinning, trying to figure out what's next.

SHARON

When the cops came,
All tough and gruff
And looking uncomfortable in their too-tight uniforms,
They strapped us in the backseats of their cruisers
Like true criminals.
Kai and Emily in one car,
Me and Cecilia in the other.

Now we're trapped in one of those rooms
With the double-sided mirrors.
I wonder, for a moment,
Whether it is a crime
To impersonate a homeless person.

If you commit a crime,
But don't know you're committing it,
Are you still busted?

EMILY

Status: 😟
Dear Hope,

   The police officers said our parents are on the way. But in
the meantime they keep coming back in. And trying to scare us
so we'll never do something "this stupid" again.

The first time, they showed us this website that lists how many sex offenders there are in the city. *Scary.* The second time, they brought in photos of all the missing and exploited kids in our state. *Scary.* The third time, they reminded us that some of our parents discovered we were missing FIVE hours ago. That for five hours they thought we'd been stolen and hurt or killed.

I couldn't stand hearing any more. I spoke up and told the police officer that none of us would EVER do something this stupid again, that we were just trying to research what it was like to be homeless for our social-issues assignment.

The police officer's eyebrows sprang up. "This was for an *assignment*?" he asked all barky. "What school do you all go to? And who is your teacher?"

Oops.

So so so so so so so so so so so unlucky,
Emily

SHARON

Cecilia has been crying for an hour.
Nonstop.
Not just a little.
She's crying an ocean.
Her whole face has puffed up.

I pat her knee and
Marinate in guilt.
This was my idea, after all.
Nothing I say or do helps.
She cries and cries and cries
Like her life is over.

Except for Cecilia's
Raggedy gasps and whimpers,
Everyone else is silent.
They all must hate me.
I wish this horrible idea
Had never ever entered
My stupid head.

KAi

Dear Frog,

On the way home from the police station, it started to pour. The rain hit the roof of our car, and it was so loud, I felt like the sky was angry with us.

I can't make myself write down what my parents said on the way home. I've let them down, big-time. There's nothing worse than seeing disappointment on my mom's face.

CHAPTER 19

CECILIA

Hola Abuelita,

I am home now, in the bathroom. My head aches from all the crying. Mami didn't enter one foot into the police station. She couldn't. She wouldn't. Instead she sent our neighbor, Señora García, who's a citizen. La Migra can't take her. I'm sure the police are suspicious—they must wonder why my mother didn't pick me up. What if they report us? My family will be ripped into pieces. This is terrible!

I like the United States . . . but I won't stay here without Mami. My home is where Mami is, not the country where I was born. I appreciate all Mami's sacrifice to get me here. But no joke—I will leave this place in a second.

The world is crying with me. It has not stopped raining.

<u>WORDS TO PRACTICE</u>
No words—I'm ripping this to shreds.

Besos y abrazos,
Cecilia

191

EMILY

Dear Hope,

I am in trouble. HUGE trouble. Mom did not speak to me the whole way home. She drove with her hands tight on the wheel, jerking it left and right to change lanes. Her knuckles turned white, and her jaw was set like it was made of cement.

When we got home, she slammed the car door shut, leaving me to sit in the car. Now I'm staring at the headrest of the front seat. And trying to decide whether to go in. I've never seen her *this* mad.

> Love and luck-I-need-you-bad,
> Emily

KAI

Dear Frog,

My parents are *unhappy* that I made such a *poor* decision.

My brother, Thomas, looked at me sideways and said he thought I was smarter than that. My sister Brianna hugged me hard like she used to when we were small, and little Jayla climbed in my lap and wouldn't let go.

All my tech privileges are revoked for the next month. I told them they don't need to punish me, because I feel bad enough myself. Dad said "nice try" on that one, but I'm not lying. I couldn't feel any worse than I do now. Mostly because of Cecilia. I have never in my life seen someone fall apart like that.

I'm so upset I can't even read.

CECILIA

Hola Abuelita,

Tonight Mami gathered my hands in hers and told me we have to move. At first I said, "But Mami . . ." Only then I stopped. I know she's right. We can't take a chance. We've moved many times before. I hate it. A new start. A new school. And just when I was making friends! I miss Emily, Sharon, and Kai already, so much that I ache.

I can't believe I did this—I brought this upon us. I have no one to blame but myself. After all Mami has done for us, I went and did something stupid that could ruin it all. What was I thinking? I'm una idiota for taking a chance.

<u>WORDS TO PRACTICE</u>
Destroying this letter. I hate the world.

Besos y abrazos,
Cecilia

EMILY

Status: 😔

Dear Hope,

This morning I figured out that I'm in even BIGGER trouble than I thought. Dad flew in from Lebanon last night. Mom called him when she thought I'd been kidnapped, and he grabbed the next plane. They found me when he was midflight, so he didn't even know I was okay until he landed.

When we picked him up at the airport, Dad hugged me so long and hard that I could barely breathe. And the stubbles on his cheeks prickled me.

He didn't talk about how disappointed he was until midway through breakfast. He said he thought I knew better than to do something like this. I concentrated on stabbing tiny bites of scrambled egg with my fork.

Mom said I'm the most important thing in her life and how she needed to know I'm safe. It sure doesn't feel like I'm the most important thing in her life.

And then my dad was all "you're usually responsible" and "we trust you" and "you gotta tell us if you're not okay."

But here's the thing. I'm *not* okay. All of a sudden I wished I hadn't been eating all that egg because it was about to come right back up along with every little detail about Kayley and Aviva and private school and Ms. Graham. So I tried to explain that if I did something great to make a difference, I thought they'd be proud?

And then they rushed in, all knee-jerk fast, to reassure me

194

that of *course* they're proud, they're *always* proud . . . and something about it irritated me.

So I stopped them and said what I really meant. That I thought Dad would make more time for me. And Mom would go back to being her regular self, the way she was before they got divorced.

Then they were totally quiet. My dad shook a salt snowstorm all over his food before he even realized.

I *think* they heard me?

I *hope* they heard me.

That was the strangest lecture I've ever had. I went out to eat, somehow got both my parents at the same table for an hour without killing each other, and kind of told them off. Bizarre.

Love and luck,
Emily

SHARON

Ms. Graham keeps the three of us in at recess.
Me, Kai, and Emily.
Cecilia is absent.
She tells us how Disappointed she is
That we took such a risk.

I try to look Ms. Graham in the eyes
But I cannot.
Because this was MY idea.

KAYLEY

Dear Ms. Graham,

Wow! Emily and her team got themselves into major TROUBLE!

Ms. Graham, are you stressed out by the whole thing? You seem stressed out for sure. It's not *your* fault that your students did something so *dumb*. I think you should give them an F. They deserve that.

Our presentation, on the other hand, will be stellar. It turns out that Blake Benson is a whiz with the computer. We're going to do a PowerPoint instead of a Poster, and he thinks he can embed all these super-cool videos into the PowerPoint. (He has <u>No Clue</u> he's my secret project.) Our research and presentation are both gonna rock, but we're not exactly sure what we're going to actually *do* to make a difference. Aviva wants to tutor little kids, and I'm doing this experiment for Blake, but I can't tell anyone about that.

Our team is meeting at my house on Wednesday. I might ask Blake to stay longer, since his mom works late and I can use the help.

This will be the best Presentation ever! Can't wait to work on it this Wednesday!

TODAY'S ACTIVITY AND PROMPT: FRIENDSHIP

Our peers can influence us in both positive or negative ways. We will begin with a discussion about the meaning of friendship and the qualities we seek in our friends.

Today's assignment is to *draw or define friendship.*

EMILY

Status: 😞

Dear Hope,

Friend: *Someone who cares about you. Someone who stands up for you when she hears someone else say something mean. Someone who's there for you no matter what. Someone who makes you feel good about yourself.*

Ms. Graham gave us fifteen minutes to write and draw. And then she said softly, "Now I want you all to think about your *own* friends. Does the definition you wrote describe your own friends? And does it describe the kind of friend *you* are to other people?"

The room got quiet all of a sudden.

I realized that I've still been thinking of Aviva as a friend. Which may be ridiculous, because that does NOT describe her. She's turned into a flimsy kite that gets blown in whichever direction the wind is going.

So if the people I *thought* were friends don't meet my own definition of friends, what does that mean? That I have no *real* friends? Or that my definition is wrong? Sharon, Kai, and Cecilia seem more like friends than the girls I considered my closest friends for most of elementary school. Although we clearly made a stupid choice together, so what does that say about us? Are we bad influences on each other?

Feeling lonely,
Emily

PS Ms. Graham stopped us again. She said we get to *decide* what kind of friend we want to be to other people. And we get to *choose* who to be friends with too.

AVIVA

Date: December 11

That whole "friendship" discussion felt like it was directed at me. I've been a rotten friend. So today I asked Bologna Betty (our lunch lady) if I could get a list of ingredients for the school pizza. She looked at me kind of funny, but she ripped off a part of the box they come in. Then I brought it to Emily. I almost couldn't watch while she read it. All I saw on her face was confusion. So I explained that there-is-no-meat-in-the-school-pizza. That Kayley lied and I thought it was a mean trick. I said I was sorry and I should have told her a long time ago. That I'm no good at speaking up.

Emily stared at her feet and nodded, but then she looked up at me and added, "But I can tell you're trying. Thank you." Then her voice got all shaky, and she said that just because we're going to be at different schools next year, that doesn't mean we can't be friends.

My throat closed up so fast that I could barely whisper "I know" without crying. I swallowed a couple of times and then I told her how I was really worried about her this weekend and how glad I am that she's okay and that I know I haven't been a very good friend to her.

It was really scary to tell Emily the truth. I worried she might get mad. But I said it anyway.

HENRY

SCENE: *Classroom—everyone working quietly.*

HENRY: *(softly)* So, Kayley, am I your friend?

KAYLEY: I like <u>quiet</u> friends. You. Are. Not. Quiet.

HENRY: *(laughs)* That was funny!

KAYLEY: *(ignores laughter)* Like Aviva. See how quiet she is?

AVIVA: *(quietly holding Kermit, as if to make Kayley's point)*

HENRY: Blake's pretty quiet.

KAYLEY: Blake's growing on me. You're my friend, Blake.

BLAKE: Uh. Okay.

KAYLEY: I'll tell you what, Henry. If you can be quiet for the next thirty minutes, I'll be your friend.

HENRY: That was funny! You're learning, Kayley. I'm teaching you well.

KAYLEY: I'm not teasing. I'm serious. Thirty minutes. Silence.

HENRY: I can do it. Just wait—you'll be begging me to talk in about five minutes.

KAYLEY: You're talking. No talking. Silence.

HENRY: *(tries not to answer)*

KAi

To the Frog,

Apparently . . . friends disappear.

Cecilia hasn't been in school at all this week.

I don't have her phone number. It's not on the class list (maybe they don't own a phone?). I don't know where she lives. What can I do?

Dear esteemed students,

The secret of a true friendship is to find a way to repair the relationship when something goes wrong. Forgiveness is a part of friendship. This also includes forgiving yourself.

Please do not forget about your mailboxes. It just takes one person to begin the process of repairing. If you're waiting for someone else to do it, you may wind up waiting forever.

Sincerely,
Ms. Graham

Dear Ms. Graham,

We are so very sorry about what happened. We didn't mean to break your trust or the trust of anyone else.

From
Emily, Sharon, and Kai

———

Dear Emily, Sharon, and Kai,

Life is about learning. Sometimes we do our best learning from our deepest mistakes.

I'm not angry. I'm just glad you are all okay.

With warm regards,
Ms. Graham

———

Dear Emily,

I will try to be a better friend to you.

From
Aviva

SHARON

Our table group slunk back from lunch
To find a sticky note
In the center of each desk.

Mine read,
"Today is a new day.
Start fresh."
Emily's was
"Look. Listen. Learn."
And on Kai's she'd written
"Breathe."

Cecilia had one too.
"Missed you today"
Was all it said.

CHAPTER 21

EMILY

Status: 😲

Dear Hope,

Mom's cell phone buzzed on the kitchen counter. Mom was painting in the studio, so I peeked at the text message. From Mrs. Barrette. *Requesting all B-5 parents come to our house tonight at 5pm to discuss Serious Concerns about our children's learning environment. Parents Only.*

My heart sank to my toes. Ms. Graham! I massively screwed up by telling the police that we'd gone to the shelter for an assignment. Now there was going to be trouble, and all because of my big mouth! Ms. Graham did NOT assign us to sneak out overnight. That was all US.

I had to DO something. I had to go to Mrs. Barrette's meeting too.

But Mom and I are trying to rebuild "trust." And since she's been making this HUGE effort to talk to me (put her work away, sit down for dinner, that kind of thing)—lying to her did not seem wise.

So I tiptoed into her studio, eyed the paint splattered all over her arms, and told her the Barrettes were hosting a meeting. That it was about Ms. Graham and I thought WE should go. I did not mention "parents only," but I didn't lie either.

Her brow furrowed like she was concerned, and she said, "Yes. We should go."

I feel like I'm heading into battle. This can only mean TROUBLE.

In desperate need of love and luck,
Emily

HENRY

SCENE: *Kayley's house for the big teacher roasting. Henry is waiting outside.*

EMILY: *(walking up with her mom)* Go on in, Mom, I'll stay and talk to Henry. *(tries to smile but looks worried)*

EMILY: What are you doing here?

HENRY: Counting the ants on the sidewalk. Waiting for my mom. Thinking of ways to get rich and famous. What are *you* doing here?

EMILY: I've got to hear what the parents are saying. This is all my fault.

HENRY: Don't blame yourself. It's more like seventy-five percent your fault. Twenty-five percent goes to these parents. They need a hobby.

EMILY: Gee, thanks. That's really comforting. I'm going to sneak in. Want to come?

HENRY: Sure. That's got to be more fun than counting ants on the sidewalk.

(Henry and Emily slip in through the front door and sit on the stairs in the hallway, not able to see who is talking.)

PARENT #1: We're sending our children to school to learn English and math, not sneak into homeless shelters, or be the subjects of social experiments!

PARENT #2: How long has she been teaching, anyway?

PARENT #3: Does it do any harm if she teaches them about social issues? As long as she gets the math and the English in there too?

PARENT #4: It's not really her fault if some of the students took this project into their own hands.

PARENT #1: Social issues and values should be taught at home, not at school.

PARENT #3: Well, what do you propose we do?

PARENT #2: Lodge a formal complaint with the school board?

HENRY: *(whispers)* Okay, maybe it's ninety percent your fault.

KAYLEY: *(winds her way down the stairs and whispers)* What are you guys doing here?

HENRY: Training to become professional spies.

KAYLEY: Come up to my room so they don't hear you.

HENRY: *(pads upstairs)* Emily's corrupting me.

KAYLEY: This is all your fault, you know. *(points her finger at Emily)*

EMILY: *(with an amazing amount of venom for someone who seems so sweet)* Who are YOU to talk?!!!!

HENRY: *(looks for an escape route)*

KAYLEY

Dear Ms. Graham,

Emily thinks she's such Hot Stuff, barging into my house and dragging Henry along. Once I got her in my room, she started asking me why I told her the cheese pizza had meat in the sauce. Can't she take a joke? She acts like it's this Huge Deal. Puh-leeze. And then she was all "we used to be friends" and "I don't understand" and "what's going on?" All I can say is that girl needs to take a chill pill.

But then out of nowhere, Henry started tap-dancing. I swear. *Tap-dancing.* Like with an imaginary cane and hat. Emily and I just stared at each other. That boy can't be serious for a second. And then Henry was all "Ladies! Let's put aside our petty differences. We've got to save our teacher from the witch hunt." Which he tried to say with an English accent.

But he had a point. I've seen my parents do this kind of thing before, and there's one thing I know for sure. This is not going to end well for you, Ms. Graham. Henry can tap-dance all he wants, but I don't think there's anything we kids can do to help you.

Henry said I should tell my parents how great you really are. But here's the thing. In my family, it doesn't matter what I want. It only matters what my parents want because they'll push and push until it happens. It's just like the river by our vacation house. From the shore it looks all gentle, like the water's hardly moving, but once I'm in, I can't swim against it no matter how hard I try. The current keeps pushing me forward. That's the way it is with my parents. It's easier to go along with the flow than it is to fight against it. Sometimes I try to convince myself that I agree, just so I won't have to disagree. There's no point in swimming against the current. I won't get anywhere. It's better to just hang on for the ride.

KAi

To the Frog,

My dad went to that big meeting at the Barrettes' last night. He left our house "pumped up" but came back dragging. He said the parents are on a witch hunt and that he tried to be a "voice of reason." He told them that it was our idea, not Ms. Graham's, and that we need to take responsibility for our choices . . . but nobody listened to him, even though he's a professor and knows what he's talking about. What if they fire Ms. Graham over this? And Cecilia has disappeared. Completely.

I wish we'd never tried to go to the shelter. It was a huge mistake. I'm so mad at Sharon, I can hardly look at her. She always thinks she knows everything, but *clearly* she doesn't.

At lunch she tried to tell me about a new idea she has to fix things. I backed away from her and yelled, "I'm done! I don't want any more of your ideas."

I hurt her feelings. Bad. Her face crumpled, and then I wished I hadn't said all that. Because of course it's my fault too.

BLAKE

Dear Parents of Room B-5,

Here at White Oak Elementary School, the safety and education of our students is our top priority. I am writing to notify you all that Ms. Graham has been placed on administrative leave, effective December 15. After winter break, the District Office will begin conducting an investigation, the results of which will be discussed at an upcoming school board meeting. Subsequently, the board will determine any disciplinary action.

Rest assured, we will work on resolving this issue as quickly as possible and getting a permanent teacher back into room B-5.

Striving toward academic excellence,
Principal Severns

EMILY

Status: 😠 😰
Dear Hope,

I can't believe it.

I feel like the school walls have crumbled in around me.

Looking around the room, I think my whole table group is feeling the same way. All the other students hate us too. They know it was *us* that screwed up, not Ms. Graham.

No matter who we tell, the grown-ups won't listen to us. Sharon, Kai, and I went to Principal Severns, but she told us this was something the "adults would handle." OMG! I'm about to rip my hair out. And Cecilia hasn't come back to school yet . . . where is she?

There's an old picture book called *Harold and the Purple Crayon*. The kid walks around all over the place, drawing things. It's like he's making up his own story as he goes. If he's falling, he draws a parachute. If he hits an obstacle, he draws an escape route. Too bad life's not really like that. Because right now, I need a purple crayon.

Feeling FRUSTRATED,
Emily

BLAKE

KAYLEY

Dear Ms. Graham,

My mother says you're in "Hot Water." She says you're on administrative leave and that's why you haven't been back in school. We've got a sub, Ms. Millbrook. She wears these big flowery dresses that hide her feet so she looks like she's gliding along the floor, like a giant float in a parade or something. She hands out worksheets all day so she can just sit there and play on her phone.

And she's *totally* freaked out by Kermit. We've had to explain to her like a thousand times that we're *allowed* to take Kermit out of his tank. It's like she thinks it's *her* classroom or something.

My mother keeps talking on the phone and forgetting I can hear. This is the first time she's gotten a teacher placed on Administrative Leave. She's Excited about it, I think. Usually when she's Excited, it sort of trickles down to me and I get Excited too. This time I feel sad and angry.

I'm not alone, though. Everyone is upset. Most kids are mad at Emily's group. They totally screwed everything up. They're the ones who should be placed on Administrative Leave. Nobody's even doing their class jobs anymore, but if they were, I'd vote to kick them off class council.

AVIVA

Date: December 18

Not only am I losing my teacher, but Ms. Millbrook is a complete imbecile with a frog phobia . . . and Cecilia hasn't been back to school. Ms. Graham always said "anyone can make a difference," but guess what? I think she's *wrong*. There is NOTHING I can do right now that will help this situation.

I asked Ms. Millbrook if I could take Kermit home for winter break. She got this surprised look on her face, like she hadn't even thought about Kermit. I bet if I hadn't suggested it, she'd have left Kermit alone in his tank for two whole weeks, and we'd come back to find him starved to death. Yikes.

The first night of Hanukkah is tomorrow, but the world feels too dark for my candles to make much of a difference. Although maybe we could all use a miracle.

KAI

To the freaking Frog,

Everyone's in pieces about Ms. Graham.

Me too.

But at least we know where Ms. Graham is. She's at home.

WHERE is Cecilia? *Where is she?* Why is no one out searching for her? I tried to ask Ms. Tildy in the front office, but she wouldn't tell me anything. She just said she couldn't share any information about another student due to confidentiality. I wanted to shake her and say, "Yeah, but *where is she?*"

I feel like I'm trying to yell but no one can hear me. HELLO? A student is MISSING! That sticky note from Ms. Graham is still stuck to her desk, taunting me with "Missed you today." I got so mad I wrote underneath, "WHERE ARE YOU?"

Real life is too hard.

We're about to start winter break, it's almost Christmas, and I'm not even excited. I still don't feel like reading. Jeeez. This has been the WORST month of my entire life.

CECILIA

Hola Abuelita,

At night, when I miss you the most, that's when my worries come. And nightmares of being separated from Mami leave me tossing and turning.

But thank you, Abuelita, for your kind words to Mami. I could tell it made her feel better to hear "No hay mal que por bien no venga." I doubt anything good could possibly come from this, but I'll try to be patient.

Thank you for talking to Mami about moving on, and getting me back into soccer. I really miss it. There isn't a lunchtime game at my new school. I like your idea of finding a different after-school team, something near our new apartment. At least that would give me something to look forward to.

Feliz Navidad, Abuelita. Hopefully, things will be better in the New Year.

<u>WORDS TO PRACTICE</u>
nightmares = *pesadillas*

Besos y abrazos,
Cecilia

CHAPTER 22

BLAKE   WINTER BREAK

SHARON

Christmas dinner stuck in my throat
Like the ham
Had turned to glue.
Mom set down her fork and tried to reassure me.
Like words could somehow
Fix this.
Like she could somehow
Smooth my worries away
With "You've learned your lesson,"
"The worst is over,"
And "At least you're all safe."

"You're wrong!"
My words tumbled out hot and heavy.
"The worst is NOW!
Ms. Graham is in huge trouble,
Cecilia is missing,
I finally had some good friends,
And now I've RUINED it!" I told her.

"Have you?" she asked.
"If there's one thing I know about you," she said,
"It's that you go to bat
For what you believe in.
The question is,
Are these friendships

And your teacher's job
Worth fighting for?"

EMiLY

Status: 🌑

Dear Hope,

Mom and I took a "girls' trip" up to Northern California over winter break. (Dad's traveling.) During all that drive time, I couldn't stop thinking about Ms. Graham. The next school board meeting is February 5th, four weeks away. We can't just sit here and do nothing! We've got to explain, we've got to do something to make people listen to us.

But this problem is a BIG problem, a grown-up problem. Is there anything WE can do about it? Out of the blue, an idea struck. We need to see Ms. Graham! She'll know how we can save her job. But I don't know where she lives, and it's not like I can ask her.

Tomorrow's the first day back at school. Maybe I'll ask Sharon and Kai to help. I guess I could ask Aviva. She put a note in my box before winter break. So . . . maybe?

We all got her into this mess.

We need to get her out.

> Love and luck,
> Emily

AVIVA

Date: January 8

First day back. I have two words: boring and sad. Even Kermit looks depressed. I suffered through the day, but after school Emily pulled me aside and shared her idea.

Then all of a sudden, I smelled Kayley's strawberry shampoo from behind me, and she kept saying, *"What? What?"* and before I knew it I was explaining to Kayley even though Emily kept elbowing me, and then it was like "oops," maybe I wasn't supposed to say that.

Only, then Kayley surprised both of us. "I'll help," she said. "I'm in. A hundred percent."

KAYLEY

Dear Ms. Graham,

We're going to get your job back. I could tell Emily didn't really want my help at first, but she's not in charge of the world, is she?

Plus I've decided the Social-Issues Project is officially back on! Our topic is still Access to Education, but I say we focus on our OWN education. If we want to learn anything this year, we've got to get you back to teach us.

PS Most of us are still writing in our journals every day . . . even though you're not here to make us. I don't know about everyone else, but writing helps me think.

SHARON

Today I found Cecilia's friends
On the far end of the playground.
"Where is Cecilia?" I asked.
One girl crossed her arms.
"They moved."
I froze. "They moved? With no warning?"

The girl looked at me like I'm stupid. "Yes.
Your little *field trip*
Could have gotten her family
In a whole lot of trouble."
I must have seemed
As confused as I felt
Because then she said,
"You don't get it."

It took me about an hour
But then it hit me
Like a fist in the face,
And I understood.
No wonder Cecilia cried a river
All over the backseat of that police car.

After school, I found Kai by the bike rack,
To tell him Cecilia had moved.
And I explained
Why.
He just stood
And scuffed his feet.

I was all, "Listen.
I messed up.
You messed up.
We messed up.

"We've got two choices.
Do nothing. Or try to help.
We may not be able to fix
Things for Cecilia.
Or for Ms. Graham.
But we owe it to them to try.
Both Emily and I
Have ideas.
You in?"

HENRY

SCENE: *Far end of the field at recess, kids clustering together.*

EMILY: What we're planning to do is against the rules. You could get in trouble. We all could. I want to make sure everyone here is making this decision on their own.

SHARON: Emily's right. No one should feel pressured. Only do this if YOU think it's the right thing to do.

KAYLEY: We're in! Come on, we've all been listening to Ms. Graham all year. All her "You get to choose the kind of person you want to be" and "You can make a difference." Let's get this started!

BLAKE: Maybe we're all one team now. It's like our two table groups merged.

KAI: Minus Cecilia.

KIDS: *(quiet, thinking about Cecilia)*

BLAKE: Right. Minus Cecilia. But like Henry said, maybe we have to stop competing and just work together.

AVIVA: Except for the Egg-Off, I don't think it was ever supposed to be a competition. Maybe we just made it one.

EMILY: Well, if we made it that way, then we can unmake it. The first step is we've got to find Ms. Graham's address.

SHARON: And we know Cecilia moved. But maybe if we go to her old place, they'll know where she is. So . . . we'll search for her address too.

HENRY: I hereby dub this adventure Operation Frog Effect. Or OFE for short.

BELL: Riiiiiiiing!

KAi

Hey there, Frog,

At first, I didn't want to talk to Sharon or go to the recess meeting. I wanted to stay sucked into my books and forget about the real world. Today my team stole the Beyonders and Fablehaven books I had in my backpack and said they'd hold them hostage unless I came to the meeting.

Yes, I'm reading again. Halfway through winter break when I was about to DIE from boredom, I picked up some old favorites, the ones with missing pages and torn covers. The stories pulled me in, and I lay in my bed reading for days. I just wandered around in a book coma and didn't think about anything real. Mom and Dad gave me a talk about how "we learn from our mistakes," and while they "*never ever ever* want to get a call like that again," all I can do is "learn and move on."

I've got the book *Wonder* on my brain again, and it makes me want to get off my butt and be the kind of person that *does something*. Maybe that's what Ms. Graham meant when she said we get to choose the kind of person we want to be.

We tried to look for Ms. Graham's address with an internet search, but it came up with way too many names. We decided the next step would be to try to find her address written down somewhere—in her desk or maybe in the front office. I looked up Cecilia's address on the internet too, but I realized I don't know her parents' first names. Jeeez!

Kayley's all about the drama, running around calling this Operation Frog Effect. She even told me she wore black today so she can sneak around without anyone seeing her. Uh, Kayley? This is not a spy mission—we're just doing what's right. Plus it's broad daylight. Get a grip.

SHARON

Here I am again,
Creeping like a criminal
Trying to right a wrong.
Hoping that having my heart in the right place
Will somehow make a difference.

Hiding in the classroom coat closet
Waiting for just the right moment . . .
When everyone is gone.
Tiptoeing up to the teacher's desk,
Ruffling through stacks of paper,
And sliding open drawers.

But . . . I cannot find a home address
Anywhere.
Next step . . . the front office.
But how will we search
Without getting caught?

I'm so glad the sneaking around
Is Emily's idea this time.
Plus we're a team again.
And that feels good.
We can't fix everything, of course.
But we can sure try.

HENRY

SCENE: *Aviva, Emily, and Henry have entered front office. Henry is not sure if he feels like a superhero or a criminal.*

EMILY: *(to Ms. Tildy, weakly)* I think I might puke.

MS. TILDY: How about you sit here in the nurse's office for a while? If you don't feel better by the time lunch is over, we'll call someone to pick you up. *(opens the drawer with the emergency contact form and pulls Emily's contact info)* Aviva, and Henry, thank you for bringing her.

(Sharon and Blake push through the front office door. Sharon has an envelope in her hand.)

SHARON: Ms. Tildy? We all signed a card for Ms. Graham.

MS. TILDY: *(glances back toward the hallway where Principal Severns's office is located, then turns back with a softer voice)* Would you like me to send it to her?

SHARON: Could you?

MS. TILDY: Yes. I'll make sure she gets it.

BLAKE: Thanks, Ms. Tildy!

(Sharon and Blake leave office. Ms. Tildy types, scrolls, and begins addressing envelope.)

KAI: *(walks into office and discreetly scoops a small frog out of his sweatshirt pocket and onto the office counter)* Ms. Tildy. I forgot my lunch. Can I call my mom?

(Kermit hops across desk counter.)

MS. TILDY: *(leaps up)* EEEK! A frog!

KAI: I'll get it! Do you have a bucket? I can trap it.

(Ms. Tildy runs to get a bucket. Henry stands up and scoots over to the open document on the computer. Takes photos of the address, then slips the phone back into his pocket. Emily flips through emergency contact forms and removes Cecilia's. Henry steps back and takes a photo of this form, then Emily slips it back in.)

KAI: *(scoops up frog with his hands)* Got it!

THE SUPERHERO SEVEN

CHAPTER 23

CECILIA

Hola Abuelita,

Our new apartment is bigger, because we decided to share a space with prima Maria and her son Josué. Mami and Maria put their money together, so they were able to get a nicer place. There's never quiet, because Josué is always blasting his music, but I don't mind. I'd rather have family around. We're taking turns cooking, and I love the smell of the polvo de chile in our kitchen.

Our neighbor has three small children, and she asked me to come over to play with them. I'd do it for free, but she offered to pay me. She calls me a "babysitter in training." I'm going to save my money.

I can't change the rules of immigration. Still, there are so many things I CAN do . . . mostly when I'm eighteen, but I can start preparing now. When I'm eighteen, I'll vote against anything that separates families. And I'll travel to visit you, Abuelita. I know it'll take a very long time to save up enough money for a trip, but I'll start now. Plus someday I want to go to law school and fight for Mami's rights and for the rights of other families like ours too.

I miss my old friends from White Oak Elementary. Do the kids from my lunchtime soccer game notice I'm gone? I wonder if my B-5 friends think of me as often as I think of them. Are Emily and Sharon still eating lunch together? And Kai? Is he still reading underneath his desk? I miss Ms. Graham too. I even miss Kermit. Maybe I'm already forgotten. They're not forgotten to me.

<u>WORDS TO PRACTICE</u>

I know I keep telling you this when we FaceTime, but your English is getting very good. I can tell you've been practicing.

forgotten = *olvidado*   babysitter = *niñera*

neighbor = *vecina*   apartment = *apartamento*

Besos y abrazos,

Cecilia

AVIVA

Date: January 13

A bunch of us met up at Pitts Park and walked together to the address on Cecilia's emergency contact form. But Sharon was right—she'd moved. And the new family didn't know to where. Kai pulled his hoodie over his head and I could tell he was feeling rotten.

I think we were all discouraged, but we moved on to our next stop, Ms. Graham's house. I worried we'd come to the wrong place, because it looked like a grandma house. It had flowers and cracked gnomes that stuck out of the weedy grass. It did not look like a place where Ms. Graham would live.

Kayley pressed the doorbell, but I hung back next to Kai and Sharon. An old lady answered the door, a golden retriever by her feet. My heart sank. We *had* stolen the wrong address. "Can I help you?" she asked. She matched the house perfectly.

My voice stuck in my throat, but Sharon told her we were looking for Ms. Graham. She smiled really big, then turned and hollered, "Bea!"

Was she Ms. Graham's mother? The grandma-lady didn't look like Ms. Graham at all. She looked like a marshmallow, but not in a bad way. Marshmallow skin—white and soft and puffy. Marshmallow legs, marshmallow arms, sugary smile.

Ms. Graham came to the door in sweat pants and a baggy T-shirt. That's not how she dresses for school at all. Her eyes got super wide, like she was surprised to see us. She just stood, all smiley for a long time, standing there like she wasn't sure what to say.

HENRY

SCENE: *Seven fifth graders standing awkwardly at their teacher's door. At first it's cringe-worthy quiet, and then, bam!, everyone's talking all over each other.*

AVIVA: We miss you, Ms. Graham!

EMILY: Ms. Graham, we are so sorry all this happened. We wish we could fix this. It's not your fault we went to that shelter!

SHARON: It's not fair that they're punishing YOU for what WE did.

KAYLEY: *(dramatic)* We HAVE to save your job.

KAI: What can we do to help?

HENRY: *(Long pause. Henry wonders if Ms. Graham even heard any of them. Blake awkwardly scuffs his feet.)*

MS. GRAHAM: Hi, guys. I really appreciate you all coming out here—I miss you too. But . . . this isn't something I can talk to you about.

AVIVA: But what about everything you taught us? Isn't there anything, even something small, that we can do to help?

MS. GRAHAM: I'm sorry, you guys, and don't worry—I'm okay—but you probably shouldn't be here. This is between me and the school board now. *(Ms. Graham's mother puts her arm around her, and then she slowly eases the door shut.)*

KIDS: *(standing frozen like icicles for a ridiculously long time)*

EMILY: What was *that*?

HENRY: Yeah, I'd been banking on a frog effect pep talk. You know, like "You can do anything," "You're the adults of tomorrow," and blah blah blah. They just don't make pep talks like they used to.

AVIVA: It's not fair. Why does the school board get to decide? They don't know Ms. Graham *or* us.

BLAKE: It's too bad *we* aren't on the school board.

HENRY: Well, why aren't we?

KAYLEY: Duh—we're kids. They don't put students on the school board!

SHARON: Why not?

KAYLEY: They just don't!

AVIVA: Maybe we should try to change that.

SHARON

A thousand thoughts
Left unsaid,
Like cartoon word bubbles
Hanging in the air.

We stood at Ms. Graham's door
Waiting
For someone to tell us what to do.
We could've waited forever.
Because this time there are no directions,
No road map, no recipe.
It's up to us to figure this out.

What I need to know

Is what did she *want* to tell us?

What did she *want* to say?

And why did she hold back?

Did we make it worse

By tracking her down?

And can we make it better?

KAi

Dear Frog,

On the walk home from Ms. Graham's, everyone started talking, saying maybe we could really try to get a seat on the school board. And if we did, then maybe then we could actually save Ms. Graham's job.

That's great, and I hope we can do it. But what about Cecilia? I'm beginning to think we'll never find her.

Maybe Sharon was wondering the same thing, because she started saying that she didn't want this whole homeless shelter thing to be for *nothing*. That we caused *all* these problems for Ms. Graham and for Cecilia and wasn't there *something* good that could come from it? Didn't we learn *anything*?

And then I was being sarcastic, and I said, "I learned my toes were about to freeze off."

Sharon stopped walking right then, and Henry bumped into her. "Well, that's something. That's definitely *something*!"

BLAKE

KAYLEY

Dear Ms. Graham,

Yesterday, when we were at your house, I'll admit that I was confused. Couldn't you have invited us in, or at least said something encouraging?

I bet you feel awful about this whole thing. At least you're not all alone, feeling sad. Your mother seemed really nice, and I can tell by the way she put her arm around you that you have a relaxed/comfortable kind of relationship. I'm guessing you don't want to get in more trouble, or make things worse, but still! What about *us*? We need you.

Here's the thing—if no one else is going to fix this, I guess I'll have to. I've watched my mother take on "Issues" for years. Not to brag, but I know how to get things done.

Plus there should *totally* be a student on the school board! (That's how we'll get your job back.) Just watch me make this happen.

EMILY

Status: 🙂
Dear Hope,

Kayley's right. If the school board gets to make the decision about Ms. Graham, then the solution is simple: We need to get student seats on that board. And we need to do it fast, BEFORE they vote on Ms. Graham. I talked to my neighbor, who's a retired principal. She said that first there will be an investigation, and then the findings will be presented at a school board meeting. So . . . there's two places we can make our voices heard—(1) the investigation and (2) the school board. Where do we start?

I've been listening to other table groups in class. Aviva keeps talking about Malala and the power of her pen. How she stood up for what she believed. I thought about Dad's job, and how he uses his writing to make a difference. I thought back to the homeless shelter, and how part of the reason I'd wanted to go was so I could write about it.

Suddenly I had this image of Harold's purple crayon, and I wondered . . . is there any way to "write" our way out of this mess? None of the grown-ups are listening to what we SAY, but what about what we WRITE? Maybe this is what Ms. Graham was saying—maybe it's exactly the kind of small thing that can make a big difference?

Love and luck,
Emily

PS Even when Kayley's just trying to be helpful in her regular Kayley way, I sort of want to find reasons to hate her. I'm working on that.

KAI

Dear Frog,

I'd like to at least *talk* to Cecilia, but I'm not sure how. I wonder if any of her lunchtime friends know how to find her. Maybe I can write a note and ask one of them if they know where to deliver it.

————————

Dear Cecilia,

We miss you at school. Do you want to meet at the library sometime? Here is my home number in case you ever want to call. 818-555-3833. My parents won't let me have social media yet, so phone is the best way. Or you can send me a note here at school.

—Kai

SHARON

Something's brewing
In room B-5.
We're cooking up
A big pot of
Something from Nothing.
I read a book with that idea once
And it reminds me of a folktale,

Where a hungry stranger
Convinces people to each
Add a bit of what they have *(nearly nothing)*
To make a soup
That will feed them all *(definitely something)*.

Each of us is
Adding our own ingredients,
Stirring it with some good intentions,
And breathing in
The bubbling aroma
Of hope.

All our "nearly nothings"
Might just make
A whole lot of
Somethings.
If we work together.

CHAPTER 24

> Dear students in Ms. Graham's class,
>
>   Everyone's invited to a kids-only meeting on Thursday night at my house. We have a top-secret plan.
>
>   —Kayley

HENRY

SCENE: *Kayley's garage, which is larger and nicer than Henry's entire apartment.*

KAYLEY: Okay, everyone! *(claps hands)* Enough chitchatting. Let's get started. We're here to find a way to get a student seat on the school board.

KAI: What makes us think anyone's gonna to listen to *us*?

AVIVA: *(in a soft voice)* We can make them.

HENRY: Uh, what? WE can't even hear *you*. Speak up, Minnie Mouse.

AVIVA: *(louder)* Let's find a way to MAKE them listen to us.

BLAKE: How?

KAYLEY: When my mother was trying to make the school lunches healthier, she sent in a formal request to put healthy lunches on the school board agenda.

SHARON: Let's do that! And maybe we could make posters to advertise what we're doing, and get people on our side.

BLAKE: I could design the posters.

AVIVA: Ooh! We could write one of Malala's quotes on them. My favorite is this one—"When the whole world is silent, even one voice becomes powerful."

KAI: Yeah! We could put them up on walls and bulletin boards. There's a place to thumbtack notices at Smoothie Smasher and also Daily Coffee. I can ask my brother, Thomas, if he can drive us around to different shops.

EMILY: We could also make a petition to show them that lots of people agree with us.

KAI: That's easy. We can stand outside the grocery store with clipboards.

EMILY: I was thinking about writing something. I'm pretty sure anyone can submit an article for the editorial section of a newspaper. I'm not sure if I can make it good enough, but if I can, maybe it'll get published?

HENRY: Awesome. And maybe we could make a video clip that we could post on my YouTube channel.

KAYLEY: You have a YouTube channel?

HENRY: Doesn't everyone?

AVIVA: My parents won't even let me watch YouTube.

HENRY: It's actually a private channel that my parents set up to show home videos to my grandparents in Taiwan. Maybe we can make a video and email it out to all the parents in our school?

KAYLEY: We can ask everyone to forward it to ten more people. And then it'll go viral!

SHARON: If we make it really catchy, it might.

HENRY: It can be sent through email and posted on internet sites. I'll be the director. Blake can help with tech stuff.

KAYLEY: Okay . . . let's make teams. If you want to be on Emily's Writing Team—go stand by the third refrigerator.

HENRY: How many fridges does a family of three need?

KAYLEY: Anyone who wants to help Blake with design should stand by the kayaks. Henry, *(gives Henry the evil eye)* no kayak comments. If you want to be on the Video Team, go stand by the skis.

HENRY: And exactly how many sports do you all do? I don't see any skydiving equipment around here. You're missing out. From what I hear.

AVIVA: *(quietly)* I think we should at least try to talk to the investigator. If the investigator doesn't think it's Ms. Graham's fault, then they won't recommend firing. Right?

KAYLEY: It's worth a try. You're in charge of that team.

AVIVA: *(squeaks)* Me?

KAYLEY: If you want to be on Aviva's Team—go stand by—

HENRY: The safe!

KAYLEY: There is no safe in the garage.

HENRY: There should be. *(looks around)*

KAYLEY: Aviva's Team—go stand by the pool table.

HENRY: Can we be on more than one team?

KAYLEY: You can be on any team you want, as long as it's not MY team. You're driving me bananas.

EMILY: I'm excited. This might work!

KAYLEY

Dear Ms. Graham,

Last night when my mother was at her PTA meeting, I invited everyone in the class for a kids-only meeting. We tossed around ideas like tennis balls. Some were completely IDIOTIC, but I figured the whole point of doing this was to get as many ideas as we could and pick the best one, so I didn't make any comments about anything.

Last night I did a really good job at one thing—being Polite. Truthfully, I would've liked to tell Aviva to shut up already about Malala (she keeps spouting off Malala quotes), and to laugh at the stupid suggestions people made, but I didn't. At first it was really hard and kind of uncomfortable, like trying to hold in a burp. But then that feeling just went away.

Ms. Graham, it made me think about your lesson on honesty and how honesty is not an excuse to be mean. Maybe being *right* isn't an excuse to be mean either. I'm pretty much always *right* (can't help it), but I'm trying harder not to rub it in everyone's faces.

PS Okay, so can I just say that me, Aviva, and Emily are pretty much leading Operation Frog Effect here? So tell me again, WHY are more men in power than women? Huh? I'm going to make it my business to change this.

———

Dear Oak Valley School Board,

We are formally requesting an agenda item for the next meeting. We would like the school board to consider adding a student seat, so that everyone's voice will be represented.

We have begun a petition, and we already have 346 signatures.

Thank you for your consideration,
The students at White Oak Elementary

CHAPTER 25

AVIVA

Date: January 19 (17 days until February 5 school board meeting)

I'm not sure how I feel about being in charge of my own team. I sort of want to hand it off to Sharon. Wouldn't she do a better job? Maybe I can recruit members who will kind of take over? I guess I'm just scared of messing this up.

I better find a way to get started. Maybe I'll bring Kermit's little carrier over next to my desk for moral support.

EMILY

Status:
Dear Dad,

I'm writing you a letter. An honest-to-god letter with pen and paper. I know, right? It's like out of a history book or something. I've decided that writing is a good way for me to voice my opinion, especially when what I'm trying to say is hard or really important. It takes practice, so here I go. There's something I've been wanting to say to you for a long time.

It was great that you came home when you were worried about me. But honestly, you feel like my uncle more than my dad. You're gone all the time. I need you here, at least some of the time. I love you and having you gone SUCKS. I'm sorry for the bad word, but I can't think of any other way to describe it.

I hope you don't get mad from this. But if I don't tell you how I feel, then you won't know.

> Love and guts,
> Emily

PS Next time we talk, remind me to tell you about this SUPER-COOL project my friends and I are working on. You'd be proud.

CECILIA

Hola Abuelita,

I joined a new community soccer team. We call ourselves Team Fusion. When I found out we practice two hours, four days a week, I was so excited. I love every part of practice—the warm-ups, the drills, the scrimmage. Everything. Because practices are longer, Mami can come watch after work. She tells me I look like I was born to run.

I told Mami how much I'm missing your cooking, and we decided that she should teach me all your recipes. Mami told me she keeps recipes mostly in her head, but we can write them down and make our own little recipe book. We'll call it *Recetas de Abuelita*.

WORDS TO PRACTICE
scrimmage = *juego de práctica*
drills = *ejercicios*

Besos y abrazos,
Cecilia

AVIVA

Date: January 22 (14 days until February 5 school board meeting)

I asked Emily, Sharon, and Henry to help me with my project. Kayley's too busy with school board stuff, so I didn't bother talking to her about it. It was a little awkward asking Emily after all that's happened this year, but I'm glad I did.

Henry makes me nervous, with all his joking around and calling me Minnie Mouse (which I've decided I don't like), but he's also fun, and I think he's a nice person. I picked Sharon because even though we don't really hang out, sometimes she and I think alike. She often winds up *saying* the things I'm *thinking*.

I kind of wondered if Sharon and Henry would take over once we started brainstorming, but they didn't. They just waited for me to tell them what to do. Henry started calling me "boss," which is *way* better than Minnie Mouse. And Sharon and Emily kept asking me what I thought, like I was really in charge.

We're all pretty sure the investigator will come to school to investigate. We're pretty sure the front office knows who's investigating Ms. Graham. And . . . we're pretty sure they won't tell us. But, like I told Blake today, there are thirty-one of us in class. Between us all, that's sixty-two ears and eyes. If we keep them open, we'll hear or see something. Kermit sat by my side the whole meeting and I'm glad I had his moral support, but honestly . . . I'm not sure I needed him.

Maybe I make an okay team leader.

Aviva, signing off

SHARON

I love
That Aviva asked me
To be on her team (!!!!!!)

I love
That she's making decisions
And Henry is calling her "boss."

I love
That Kai wrote a note

For Cecilia.
I offered to deliver it
To her friends.
I am not sure
How I feel about Emily
And Aviva reconnecting.

I kind of thought Emily
Had moved on to me.
But maybe I was just
Her rebound friend.
Holding the place
Until she and Aviva could make up.
Is this the kind of friendship that can stretch to three?

EMILY

Status: 😵
Dear Hope,

It's been kind of fun to watch Aviva get so into being the team leader. She sat there, with Kermit by her side, and she seemed almost . . . confident? Like the way she used to seem when it was just the two of us at her house. I hardly ever see her be that way at school.

Things are shifting. It's strange. Our two table groups are no longer enemies (competing against each other to have the best projects), but teammates. And Aviva and I are good again. Not 100%, but like at least 80%. It's like whatever was broken between us is now healing.

Aviva assigned everyone in class to watch out for the investigator. We're all taking extra bathroom and water breaks just to get more time wandering around. So far, I've found five adults I didn't recognize. One was an instructional aide from the special education class. I found a speech therapist and a school psychologist. Two parent volunteers. I'll keep looking.

Sharon joined my WRITING team, and we found this blog called KidChat. Kids get to write posts about real-world issues that affect them. We wrote an article about students on school boards. We used a thesaurus and reworked it a whole bunch of times . . . and then we submitted it. Fingers crossed!

KIDCHAT BLOG POST

Question of the Day: Should Students Sit on School Boards?
by Emily Thompson and Sharon Dukas

Fun Fact: Do you know that we spend an average of 6.24 hours in school every day, and an average of 181 days in school each year?

Not-So-Fun Math: This is 1,129.44 hours at school every year. And we're in school for 13 years if you count kindergarten, so that's 14,682.72 hours of our childhoods. Plus homework time, college, and maybe even graduate school? Total calculation = a ton of time.

So why aren't we, the students, consulted about our own education? Why don't we get to pick the school lunches? Why don't we get to choose what we learn about? Why aren't we part of the hiring and firing of teachers?? And why aren't we given seats on school boards?

Here in Southern California, at White Oak Elementary, fifth-grade students are advocating for the addition of a student seat on their school board. They take issue with the idea of adults making all the decisions. They believe their voices should be heard.

Back to our original question, "Should students sit on school boards?"

The answer depends on whether or not you care what your students think.

Weigh in here:
- Click here to add your name to their petition.
- Click here if you think school boards should have at least one student seat.
- "Share" or "like" if you agree.

SHARON

Kai and I cannot forget about Cecilia.
We know WHY
She disappeared into a poof of smoke.

Like a magician's trick gone wrong.
We just don't know WHERE.

So I bring Kai's note
And sit with Cecilia's friends at lunch.
I promise, cross my heart,
Hope to die, and on my mother's life
That I won't tell anyone, that I have no bad intentions,
That she is my friend,
And I just want to make sure she's okay.

Guess what?
Now I know where to find her.
I can deliver Kai's note
Myself.
I think I'll wait
To tell Kai.
It'll be a surprise.

CECILIA

Hola Abuelita,

    I've been stashing all my babysitting money in an envelope.
I showed Mami and told her what I planned to do with my savings. She hugged me tight. "Abuelita feels your love, mija," she told me. This made me smile.

I've been to the park every day this week, Abuelita! I've been practicing my drills and improving my speed. My feet are already faster. Then I lie in the grass and the blades tickle the back of my neck. I keep my eyes closed, but the sun is so bright that it shines through my lids. Saving this babysitting money makes me feel hopeful, Abuelita. It makes me feel like I'm DOING something, not just waiting and worrying.

Today my eyes snapped open when I heard someone call my name. It was Sharon, my friend from my old school. I sat up and gave her a quick hug. She told me that she's been worried about me.

My throat tightened, and I hoped I wouldn't cry in front of her. I explained that we left quickly, and we didn't have time for goodbyes. She told me, "Cecilia. SO much has happened since you left. Ms. Graham got in big trouble. They're trying to fire her."

All I could say back was "Seriously?" I couldn't believe it. How could they want to fire a teacher who actually made learning fun? That makes me sad, and a little mad.

Sharon gave me a folded-up note from Kai and told me everyone was worried about me and they were so sorry if they caused problems for me and my family. Sharon pressed the edges of her sweatshirt against her eyes.

Then she said there was a school board meeting coming up, and invited me to come. Oh, Abuelita! I want to see my old friends, and thank Kai for his kind note. I don't think Mami will mind. There are too many goodbyes in my life. I need more hellos.

<u>WORDS TO PRACTICE</u>

goodbyes = *despedidas*

babysitting = *cuidado de niños*

grass = *pasto*

I'm adding a word that's not in my letter, but it's one I want you to know because I'm feeling it right now!

joy = *alegría*

Besos y abrazos,

Cecilia

BLAKE

CHAPTER 26

EMILY

Status: 😳
Dear Hope,

Whoa.

I'm taking a breath. I'm writing this down. I'm not sure if I believe it. The KidChat blog is running our "Students on the School Board" post! They asked us to make some small changes, but Mom said she'll help us. I'm a REAL writer now! Just like my dad. If getting something published always feels this good, I can see why Dad's so into it. They even want Sharon and me to send our photos in for the post.

We're a teeny tiny bit excited. Okay, truth—we're a WHOLE LOT excited. We're already planning our next post. One on Ms. Graham, of course. And maybe later we'll do one about the need for more homeless shelters. I know there's no guarantee that KidChat will want another one of our articles, but why not try?

Love and luck,
Emily

KAi

Hey, Frog!

I haven't worked this hard on a project in my entire life. Funny thing . . . it doesn't even feel like work. I'm on the Design Team. Blake and I have been playing around with different images.

We've got a theme now, at least. We like Malala's quote, "When the whole world is silent, even one voice becomes powerful." But we didn't want to use those words exactly. Instead we came up with something similar. Our poster slogan will be "Everyone deserves a voice."

Plus we've been passing around our petition for a student seat. Guess how many we have so far? More than a thousand. It's because of the internet. Emily's mom helped her set up something where people can sign electronically and forward to someone else. My mom and dad have shared it with their university department, and their education students, and all the parents are getting really into it now, and posting it (and reposting it) on social media, which kind of snowballs, you know? Plus Emily and Sharon's blog post links to the petition, so I bet we'll get more signatures soon.

Sharon pulled Cecilia's "missed you today" sticky note off her desk, and it'd been there so long it left some glue residue on the table. I was just about to get mad at Sharon for it, but she caught my eye and said, "I'm working on it, Kai. Trust me."

HENRY

VIDEO

Scene: Camera pans slowly across a fast-food drive-through.

VOICE-OVER (AVIVA): Would you order food without looking at the menu?

Scene: Camera pans slowly across voting polls.

VOICE-OVER (SHARON): Would you pass laws without taking a vote?

Scene: Camera zooms in to a meeting with adults, backs facing camera.

VOICE-OVER (BLAKE): Would you run a PTA without parents . . .

VOICE-OVER (KAI): . . . or a staff meeting without staff?

Scene: Image of jail cell and hands holding on to the bars.

VOICE-OVER (KAYLEY): Even criminals get to speak up in court. That's because we live in the United States of America.

Scene: Camera zooms in on White Oak Elementary School.

VOICE-OVER (EMILY): Then how can you have a school board without students? Think about it. We deserve a voice.

Written words sliding across screen: IF YOU AGREE, LET YOUR SCHOOL BOARD KNOW.

Scene: Four images slide in. (1) image of phone, (2) image of email, (3) image of pen and paper, (4) image of a meeting

VOICE-OVER (ALL STUDENTS TOGETHER): Because EVERYONE deserves a VOICE.

CECILIA

Hola Abuelita,

Coach is playing me as a striker. She says my speed and strength make this a good position for me. In today's game at the end of the second half, the score was 5 to 5, and then I scored, almost from midfield! YESSSS!

I heard cheering from my team and I looked over. Mami stood clapping, and next to her was Ms. Graham! She stood with a big dog on a leash, shading her eyes. I was SO tempted to run right out of the game and go talk to her. I was afraid she'd leave and I wouldn't get a chance to find out what happened to her.

I tried my best to focus on the game, and when it ended, I jogged to her side. "Hi, Ms. Graham," I said, all breathless.

She smiled and said hi back and told me I've gotten faster. I had so many questions to ask her, but I didn't know where to start. Instead I told her that I missed her. (My new teacher is *so* boring.) She said she'd missed us too, and then she seemed like she was in a hurry to leave. I'm definitely going to that school board meeting.

midfield = *medio campo*

                                    Besos y abrazos,
                                    Cecilia

KAI

Hey, Frog!

I saw Ms. Severns walking around with this short, dressed-up lady (wearing a district office badge). I swear she looked just like the evil Umbridge from Harry Potter, and I could tell she wanted Ms. Severns to know she was important.

The investigator! I found her!!!!

Let me just say, she did not seem the open-minded type. I turned and took a long drink at the fountain so I could listen a little. Ms. Severns's voice was all high-pitched. Seeing my principal nervous tells me that my gut feeling is right on.

This investigator means trouble.

KAYLEY

Dear Ms. Graham,

So much is happening! The school board meeting is tonight. The student seat is an official Agenda Item, and we've got over three thousand signatures on our petition. Emily and Sharon's KidChat blog post has gotten six hundred and fifty-seven shares, and Henry's YouTube link has been viewed more than a thousand times. We're gonna crush it!

Aviva's plan actually worked. Not that I doubted her. Okay, maybe I did. But the girl pulled it off! We found the Investigator, and she had her name right there on a badge. She talked to the principal, and other teachers, and she pulled out a few of us students to talk to individually. We hadn't really prepped for that part. Hopefully nobody screwed it up.

Aviva and Emily are buddy-buddy again, but Blake's taking up a ton of my time anyway, so it's okay. He's actually turning into a friend (!!!).

AVIVA

Date: February 5 (0 days until February 5 school board meeting)

We're NOT ready! Need More Time!

The investigator talked to a handful of kids. Not *me,* though. She didn't talk *to me.* And I really had *a lot to say.*

I felt almost sick about it. Through the window I could see the investigator walking back toward the parking lot. Leaving already? But what if I don't even get a *chance* to talk to her? What if she shares her findings tonight, before we even get a student seat on the board? Then everything we've done will have been for *nothing.*

Maybe I was talking under my breath, because Henry was all, "Me neither. And you *know* I've got a lot to say." I was a little confused because I didn't know I'd been talking out loud in the first place, but then he was like, "You go, boss. You can do it."

So before I knew it, I was waving my hand in the air, like my bladder was about to burst. Only Ms. Millbrook kept typing on the computer, not even glancing up. The investigator shrank in the window as she edged farther and farther away, and Henry nudged my elbow, so I scrambled up to Ms. Millbrook's desk. "Can I go to the bathroom, please?" I asked, and I'm pretty sure I looked desperate, because I sure felt that way.

Ms. Millbrook glanced up real slow and looked at the clock, and it reminded me of that scene from *Zootopia* when the sloth is telling a joke in the slowest-possible-way. "I have to go *badly*," I added. But then she was all, "It's almost recess. Can't you wait?"

I shot a glance out the window again. The investigator pulled her rolling briefcase near the last portable building. Then all of a sudden, Henry was behind me, whispering to Ms. Millbrook. "Ms. Millbrook? Aviva is too shy to tell you, but she has a *stomach issue.* I sit right next to her. I should know."

And Ms. Millbrook's forehead bunched, and she ushered me off, and if I wasn't about to cry, I might have burst into hysterical laughter. *Stomach issue?* He might as well have said "explosive diarrhea" or "toxic gas."

But it did the trick, because she handed me our stuffed-animal-frog bathroom pass, and I bolted out the door, down the hall, after the investigator, after her clickety-clicking heels. For a split second, I was grateful for all that relay race practice, because I've never run so fast.

"Wait, wait!" I yelled as I ran, which I know is not polite, and especially not-the-way-to-talk to a grown-up at school. But the investigator kept walking.

I barreled past the kindergarten quad, nearly tripping over a backpack, and then some kinder-aide stepped in front of me with her mad-teacher-of-small-children voice: "There is NO RUNNING in the halls!" And believe it or not, I just dodged her, and kept racing toward the investigator.

"WAIT!" I yelled again. The investigator whirled around, all surprised, and she looked like the kind of person who wouldn't believe my stuffed frog was a bathroom pass, and I thought I might be about to faint from stress and lack of oxygen, so I figured I'd better talk real fast before I passed out or got sent to the principal (whichever might happen first).

"Ms. Mervin," I read her name from her badge, "you can't leave yet—you didn't talk to me, you didn't hear what I had to say." She gave me an impatient, I-don't-have-time-for-this sigh, but I just took a deep breath and kept on talking. "*Please* don't decide about Ms. Graham at the school board meeting tonight. You have to hear from all of us first."

She straightened up, her eyebrows bunching like angry caterpillars. "Excuse me?" Only she'd clearly heard, because she went on to say, "I cannot discuss ongoing investigations." With every word, her mouth lay flatter and flatter, which did not give me a good feeling. I could tell I'd irritated her. "I'll be presenting at next month's meeting."

And she turned to continue click-clicking past the field and toward the gate, but I still hadn't told her what I wanted to say. So I ran after her, letting my words just spew out. "Ms.

Graham's a good teacher—she taught us to think for ourselves, and just because some of us made a mistake doesn't mean she was wrong to teach us that way. What's worse—teaching us to think and helping us learn from our mistakes, or not teaching us to think?"

Ms. Mervin didn't nod or smile or slow down her clickety-clicking footsteps, but I kept chattering all the way to the parking lot gate.

SHARON

Our Something from Nothing Soup
Is bubbling over,
Making a mess.
Kids are panicking
That they somehow
Screwed up
When the investigator
Questioned them.
Aviva's stressed—
Wondering if she said too much . . .
Or too little.

Me, I'm trying to stay calm
Walking home after school,
Stopping to skip rocks at the lake.
Watching the ripples,

The way the water curls away
With each plop or plunk,
Disturbing the calm surface,
And rippling as far
As the eye can see.

How much are these ripples like life?
None of us thought about
How our choices
Could impact Ms. Graham's job
Or Cecilia's life.
And now our Plan—
To save our teacher,
Reconnect with our friend,
And collect warm socks,
These are ripples too.

I've learned something:
Once our rocks are thrown, pebbles or not,
We cannot stop the ripples.
They have a life of their own.

CHAPTER 27

BLAKE

HENRY

SCENE: *Seven students hold hands, facing a row of adults behind a circular desk. The students pass a microphone around. Outside there are tons of students and other supporters holding up "Because Everyone Deserves a Voice" signs for people to see as they walk in. There's a local news crew in the back of the room, filming everything. The room has gotten so crowded that people are standing along the back wall, and the room is starting to smell like B.O.*

KAYLEY: If the purpose of a school board is to make decisions that support students in schools, then you need to know what students want.

SHARON: There are five members on your school board. If you added one student, there's no way the student could outvote you. What's the harm in having a student voice?

STERN LADY: We have an odd number of school board members so that we don't get stuck in stalemates.

HENRY: *(smiles, holds back a joke—the word "stalemate" sounds funny)*

KAI: You could have two students on the school board. Then there would be seven members and you'd still have an odd number.

EMILY: Adults don't give kids enough credit. We can make responsible decisions. And we deserve to have a voice, especially when decisions are being made about our education or our TEACHERS.

HENRY: *(hopes no one is thinking about the decision Emily's team made that was NOT responsible)*

STERN LADY: Your input will be taken into consideration. When you're done presenting your case, we'll take a vote in a closed session.

SKINNY MAN WITH TIE: *(leans into microphone)* Please know that we've seen your petition and we are aware that the community supports you.

AUDIENCE: *(Claps quietly at first, then a bunch of kids stand up and cheer. Blake's smiling so wide that his face might crack.)*

SKINNY MAN: I haven't seen the boardroom this full in . . . well, ever.

AUDIENCE: *(Chuckles and cheers. Emily hugs Aviva.)*

SKINNY MAN: So, regardless of our decision here, please know we are impressed with your commitment and courage.

HENRY: *(thinks this is not a good sign)*

STERN LADY: Thank you for your time.

STUDENTS: *(file out slowly into the waiting room)*

KAYLEY: Wow. Henry, you were serious that whole meeting.

HENRY: Can I breathe now? That was hard.

KAYLEY: Seriously, Henry. You did great.

HENRY: I swallowed seven different burps, and I counted at least three different flavors.

KAYLEY: *(grins)* Was one of them shrimp-flavored?

HENRY: Yes! One was most definitely shrimp-flavored.

KAI: Wait. Is that Cecilia over there? In the back?

SHARON: I invited her. I told you to trust me, didn't I?

BUNCH OF KIDS: Cecilia!!!!! *(run up and hug her)*

KAI

Hey, Frog!

Cecilia came tonight!!!!! And she hugged me.

And told me she missed me. That she got my letter, and she'd love to go to the library sometime. She wrote her address on my hand. I don't have words to explain how I am feeling. All I can say is my chest wants to float up to the ceiling like a helium balloon.

EMILY

Status: 😊 🤣 😊

Dear Hope,

Today was the BEST DAY!

KCAL 7 filmed segments from the school board meeting. I wonder if they caught any of us kids on camera?

Cecilia showed up at the school board meeting and I've never seen everyone so excited. I'm SO glad she's okay. Afterward, Mom took a bunch of us out for ice cream (Cecilia too). While we were licking our cones, Mom got a text from Mrs. Barrette. The school board approved two student seats!!!!!! We all did the happy dance in circles around the ice cream shop. Henry even stood on his chair to boogie, which made us laugh.

They'll hold elections in three weeks, so that the student members can attend the next meeting. Which HAPPENS to be when they plan to vote on Ms. Graham. We might actually be able to pull this off!

When I got home tonight, Dad and I Skyped. I told him all about the school board, and he said nice things about my Kid-Chat blog post (which he read). Then he took a deep breath and said he got my letter (I almost forgot about it!). He thanked me for being so honest. He said he'd make it a point to take more local assignments. And he wants to spend more time with me on school holidays and summers. Wow. This speaking up for myself actually works. I'm TOTALLY gonna run for school board.

Love and luck,
Emily

SHARON

We did this.
WE did.
Plus, not that it matters—
Okay, it TOTALLY does,
But this week I found four
Letters in my mailbox.

Dear Sharon,

Are you free on Saturday? Mom says I can invite friends to the movies. I'd like to invite you, Aviva, and Cecilia.

From Emily

Dear Sharon,

We haven't hung out too much, but I wanted to tell you that I've always admired that you can say what you think. Thank you for helping my team.

From Aviva

Dear Aviva,

Thank you for your letter. You know what's funny? I've always admired you too, but for the opposite reason. I feel like you always pick your words so carefully, and wait for the right time to say them. You also know when to let things go.

Looks like maybe we'll be going to the movies together soon. Yay!

From Sharon

CHAPTER 28

Blake

KAYLEY

Dear Ms. Graham,

You're going to think I'm losing it, but I'm not going to run for the school board elections. It doesn't feel fair to take a spot if I'm changing schools next year anyway. I know there are no students on the school board at La Ventana, but (not trying to sound conceited) I'll just propose it. I DO know how to get things done. I'm a Barrette, after all.

I talked to my parents last night. I told them I don't like when they step into my life and make huge Tornados! Did they stop for one second and think how I'd feel if they got my teacher placed on Leave? They totally looked surprised, but they listened.

I've never done that before, not with them. It felt good.

Also, Saturday late afternoon, Emily called my house. She said they were all going to the movies and I could join them if I wanted. At first, I got all paranoid, because it's not like Emily and I are friends anymore. But then I decided if I didn't go, the three of them would probably spend the whole time gossiping about me. And guess what? I had Fun.

AVIVA

Date: February 10 (23 days until March 5 school board meeting)

Emily, Sharon, Cecilia, Kayley, and I went to see a movie. Emily sat next to me, and we both totally cracked up at all the funny parts (and even only medium-funny parts), and then couldn't stop laughing until our stomachs hurt. It's so great to be silly with Emily again. I thought it'd be weird, hanging out with Kayley *and* Emily. It was, at first. But after a while, it was fine again.

I just about fell out of my chair when Kayley told me she *wasn't* running for the school board. Students from all over the district can run, but this first term I hope two kids from White Oak Elementary School get elected. It seems only fair, since we did all the work.

I'm bummed that Kayley and I are leaving the school district next year, but Kayley thinks we can get on the school board at La Ventana. Kayley thinks she can do anything. The strange thing is that she's usually right.

I started thinking. . . . Maybe *I* can do anything too. Kayley has guts—she goes for what she wants. Maybe that's what I have to do too. So tonight, I worked up my nerve to sit Ima and Aba down for a talk. This is what I said—that sometimes I don't think they really hear me. I know they want what's best for me, but that my thoughts and feelings need to matter too. Please-please-please could I at least be part of the decision about middle school? In seven years I'll be an adult. Maybe we could visit both La Ventana and Sequoia Middle School and then decide together.

Good news: They listened to me without interrupting.

Bad news: They said they needed to think about it (which usually means no).

SHARON

To be honest
I was a little miffed
That Emily invited Kayley
To the movies.
But surprisingly, it turned out okay.

Emily sat right smack in between
Aviva and me.
She shared her red licorice,
I shared my popcorn,
And I decided that maybe
This IS a friendship that can stretch
To three. Or even four.
Emily, Aviva, Cecilia and me . . . that works!
The jury's out on Kayley, though.
Only time will tell.

CECILIA

Hola Abuelita,

   Kai brought a stack of valentines to my apartment. I guess he collected them from my classroom mailbox. I was totally surprised, and I don't know why, but it made me want to cry a little, even though I didn't feel sad.

WORDS TO PRACTICE
valentines = *las tarjetas del día de San Valentín*
These are cards that celebrate *el día de amor y amistad.*

Besos y abrazos,
Cecilia

SHARON

So there are RULES
About Valentine's Day.
Bring. A. Card. For. Everyone.
Don't. Leave. Anyone. Out.
And for years,
I've gotten cheapo
Mass-produced
Folded pieces of cartooned paper
With scribbled signatures.

But this year,
I found five REAL valentines
With REAL messages.
I think this is the first year
That people actually
Know me
Well enough to write
Something meaningful.
I'll take it.

CHAPTER 29

EMILY

Status: ☺
Dear Hope,
   OMG! OMG! OMG!

You won't believe it!

Two amazing things happened. Not only was I elected to the school board, but we might be on TELEVISION tonight! Yippee!

After school, KCAL 7 (yes, for real!) interviewed Sharon and me about our KidChat blog post for a local-interest story, following up on the news clip from the last school board meeting. They needed our parents' permission (of course they said yes!) and asked us to stay after school for an interview.

OMG—there was an actual microphone and a real live camera operator (eek!). The reporter asked a few questions about the blog post, but then Sharon . . . she's so BRAVE . . . she leaned right into the camera and said, "We're working on another blog post right now. This one's about our teacher, Ms. Graham. We'd like to raise awareness and get her job back!"

And then the reporter was all, "Tell us more about that."

And Sharon jumped right in with all that happened, and how it's not fair, and Ms. Graham being such a great teacher, and now that we've got students on the board, maybe we've got a chance at keeping one of the best teachers in the world. WOW.

I know the news doesn't run every part of what's filmed, but I bet there's a good chance they'll show at least a part of the interview. Can't wait to tell Dad. Maybe Mom will let me stay up late to watch the eleven o'clock news.

Love and guts,
Emily

PS It might seem strange that I invited Kayley to the movies, after all she's done to me. Here's the thing—if I get to choose who I want to be, I just want to be the kind of person who never chooses to leave anyone out.

SHARON

Mom and I went for a walk before dinner.
She linked her arm in mine
And told me she was proud of me.
For not giving up on friendship,
For not giving up on what's right,
For knowing what's worth fighting for . . .
And what things to let go.

When I asked her if I could invite
A few friends over for pizza
She said, "Sure thing, sweet thing!"
And hugged me.

I finally have some true friends.
People I TRUST.
I feel like I've been waiting to find them
Forever.
Who knew they were right under my nose the whole time?

KAi

Hey, Frog!

Guess what? I found out that Cecilia's new place is two miles from my house. I can walk it in twenty-seven minutes. I can run it in fifteen. I can skateboard it in twelve. Yesterday I half-ran and half-walked, so it took me twenty-two.

Next Wednesday, Cecilia and I are meeting at the library to do homework and read. She mostly likes realistic fiction, but I bet even the first chapter of Harry Potter will get her hooked on fantasy. She said she'll read one of my favorites, and I promised to read one of hers.

As for Ms. Graham, it's coming down to the wire, because the school board meeting is in three days. But after all the excitement recently, the world seems strangely quiet.

This makes me nervous.

CHAPTER 30

HENRY

SCENE: *School board meeting. Blake and Aviva's image with Malala's quote is everywhere. It's on hundreds of flyers that were placed on every seat in the boardroom. It's been emailed and posted on social media, and hand-delivered to a certain news station, which has apparently come to cover this event. KCAL 7 reporting crew is stationed throughout the room. Ms. Graham is sitting in the front row, wearing a stiff suit and looking serious.*

Agenda Topic: Administrative Leave Presentation/Decision (B. Graham)

INVESTIGATOR: In review, I conducted meticulous interviews with students, teachers, parents, and staff. After careful analysis of data, one clear theme rose to the surface. Clearly, Ms. Graham's teaching methods are "outside the box."

HENRY: But interesting . . . right? Sure to grab kids' attention? Maybe inspiring?

STERN LADY: Ahem. I'll remind our newest board members that our policy is to listen to the report in full before any comments and before a vote.

HENRY: Got it. *(sits on hands)*

INVESTIGATOR: Back to my findings. The clear theme that arose is that Ms. Graham has been teaching these children to think . . . and speak . . . for themselves. *(pauses and looks at Aviva, who looks like she's about to burst)* To be active learners rather than passive recipients. With this method, there have been complications, for sure, ones that a more seasoned teacher might have avoided.

EMILY: *(grabs Henry's hand under the table)*

INVESTIGATOR: In my interview of Ms. Graham, she provided me with extensive documentation, research articles, and her own personal notes from class. While there were some passionate voices in support of Ms. Graham, the most convincing rationale was her own. It is clear her methods were well thought out and research based. For this reason, my recommendation to the school board is to provide master teacher mentoring for a full year—

HENRY: *(squeezes Emily's hand; Ms. Graham still has a serious face)*

INVESTIGATOR: . . . And for Ms. Graham to resume her teaching position as soon as possible.

HENRY: YES!!! *(cheers!—stops; looks around)* Oops! Sorry.

EMILY: *(stands up and starts clapping)*

KIDS FROM B-5: *(jumping up and down in the audience, whooping, and some kids happy-crying, the kind that surprises you while you're smiling)*

AUDIENCE: *(Except for a few crotchety people in the back, everyone stands up and starts clapping. Henry considers tap-dancing but decides against it.)*

EMILY: *(Speaks to Henry. The crowd is so loud only he can hear her.)* I can't believe it. They listened. WE DID THIS.

HENRY: We really did!!!! *(Thinks he might happy-cry too, and knows he'd be okay with that. A bunch of B-5 students jump out of their seats and run up to Ms. Graham.)*

SKINNY MAN WITH TIE: *(waits for crowd to settle down)* The excitement is refreshing, if you ask me. I hope you all stay this engaged for our next topic, which has to do with standardized testing.

HENRY: *(too excited to groan, wipes a happy tear from his eye)*

BLAKE

AVIVA

Date: March 5

Tonight it felt like we were in the center of a movie (and we kind of were, with the news station filming the whole time). When we found out Ms. Graham was getting her job back, we screamed and jumped and cheered and everything was so loud I could hardly think but it was *wonderful-wonderful-wonderful!*

Ima and Aba came to the school board meeting to support our team. The whole night they kept sneaking peeks at me, and I wondered if maybe I had food stuck in my teeth or something. On the drive home, I found out why.

They said I'm turning into such a remarkable-young-woman. With a good head-on-her-shoulders, and a passionate soul.

Ima twisted around in the front seat so that she could see my eyes. She said they've been thinking about our conversation. That they think I'm right—that we DO need to make this decision together. Ima suggested we set up appointments to go visit a few different schools, including Sequoia Middle School (where Emily will be going) and La Ventana. Aba added that they *cannot/will not* send me to any school they feel is unsafe, but that they *can try/will try* to be open-minded.

I wanted to climb right over the seats and hug them. But I didn't, for obvious seat belt–related reasons. Plus, I didn't want to make this a big deal. (Even though I kind of feel like it is.)

KAI

Whoop-whoop, Frog!

Can't wait! *Ms. Graham is coming back!!!*

Tonight was tight! The KCAL 7 News team caught a bunch of us midhug. We straightened up real fast. I was smiling all over the place, but I gave an extra-nice smile for the camera. Then the reporter caught sight of Ms. Graham. "Ms. Graham, is there anything you'd like to say to our viewers?"

She stood there for a moment, like maybe she didn't know what to say. But then she leaned into the microphone. "Just this—I'm eager to get back in the classroom and work with my extraordinary students."

Us too, Ms. Graham. Us too.

CHAPTER 31

HENRY

SCENE: *Ms. Graham's classroom on her first day back. Nobody can believe this is really happening.*

KAYLEY: Say something, Ms. Graham!

HENRY: *(cups hands around mouth)* Speech! Speech! Speech!

MS. GRAHAM: *(stands in the front of the classroom, wearing her frog-tastic socks and smiling)*

AVIVA: *(yells in an unusually loud voice)* We missed you, Ms. Graham!

EVERYONE: *(turns to look at Aviva in shock)*

HENRY: I've never heard you talk that loud in my life!

MS. GRAHAM: *(all choked up)* I missed you too. I'm so glad to be back.

EMILY: Ms. Graham! Are you crying?

To my esteemed fifth-grade students,

I am not ashamed of crying in front of you, but I was too choked up to say what I wanted to say.

For that reason, I'm putting it into a letter. I am incredibly touched by your efforts. You didn't sit back and wait for someone else to fix the situation. You stood up and made a difference yourselves. It has been an honor to watch you mature and find your voices this year.

Class party tomorrow. We have plenty to celebrate.

With the warmest of regards,
Ms. Graham

CECILIA

Hola Abuelita,

The town of White Oak has the most beautiful library in the world, with high ceilings and stained-glass windows. Kai and I meet next to the water fountain and then read together, trading books. Both our elementary schools feed into the same middle school, so next year we'll be together again. How's that for luck?

Our recipe book is halfway done. We'll mail a copy along with the soccer photo album that Mami's been making. Love you mucho!

I remember what you said before, "No hay mal que por bien no venga." You said that sometimes the good that comes out of something bad isn't clear to us at first. I'm not sure if that's true, but I think maybe it's a nice way to look at the world.

<u>WORDS TO PRACTICE</u>
library = *biblioteca*
water fountain = *bebedero*

Besos y abrazos,
Cecilia

EMiLY

Status: 😅 😵 😌 👻 😀 😎 😊
Dear Hope,

I can't wait to celebrate with Ms. Graham tomorrow!!! A bunch of us are coming in early to help set up for the party.

I got to thinking about *Harold and the Purple Crayon* again. Even though I don't go around drawing my world with a purple crayon, maybe I still get to make up my own story?

I guess for that reason, middle school isn't looking so bad. Yippee!

Love and guts,
Emily

HENRY

SCENE: *Class party, celebrating Ms. Graham's triumphant return to the classroom and Henry's never-ending awesomeness. Serving lemonade, honey wheat pretzels, cheese pizza, shrimp chips, and snickerdoodle cookies.*

HENRY: Nothing goes with lemonade like some good shrimp chips.

KAYLEY: Just ignore him until he says something relevant.

HENRY: Salty and crispy. With a slight fishy taste. What more could you ask for?

KAYLEY: Ms. Graham, would I get in trouble if I dumped my lemonade on Henry's head?

MS. GRAHAM: No comment.

SHARON: Maybe we can come up with a new project.

HENRY: Let's pick something easy. How about world peace?

MS. GRAHAM: There's still three months left of the school year . . . I bet you all can come up with something. Based on what you've accomplished thus far, I doubt anything's out of your reach.

HENRY: Awww. Even Kermit's getting misty-eyed. Long live the frog!

KAYLEY: *(laughs)*

HENRY: What? What's so funny?

KAYLEY: YOU are, remember?

HENRY: Thank you, thank you. *(small bow)* Finally! My humor is appreciated.

MS. TILDY: *(enters classroom, carrying a huge box)* Excuse me, Ms. Graham. I'm sorry to interrupt. But you've received some letters. I've been collecting them for you. *(Heaves box down on a table. The box is overflowing.)*

SHARON: WOW.

MS. TILDY: Yes. *(Appears distracted by Kermit. Henry hopes she doesn't recognize the frog from when he was released in her office.)* Ahem. I think perhaps the news coverage has gotten you some attention. Apparently, your students aren't the only ones you've made think.

BLAKE: You're famous!

MS. TILDY: Oh, and a few of the letters are addressed to your class, Ms. Graham. I guess they've caught some people's attention too. Couldn't imagine why? *(smiles and winks at class)*

MS. GRAHAM: What can I say? They're pretty frog-tastic. *(gestures to classroom)* Look at these walls.

KAYLEY: What? *(modestly)* No biggie—we just put up a few affirmations.

BLAKE

IF YOU'D LIKE TO LEARN MORE . . .

About the Malala Fund and Malala Yousafzai's amazing work:

Check out her website: malala.org

About Malala herself:

Yousafzai, Malala, and Patricia McCormick. *I Am Malala: How One Girl Stood Up for Education and Changed the World*. New York: Little, Brown and Company, 2014.

About the issue of homelessness:

National Alliance to End Homelessness: endhomelessness.org
National Center for Homeless Education: nche.ed.gov/index.php
National Coalition for the Homeless: nationalhomeless.org
Strategies to End Homelessness: strategiestoendhomelessness.org

About other creative ways to address poverty:

Heifer International: heifer.org
UNICEF: unicef.org
The Water Project: thewaterproject.org

About fun ways people are spreading kindness:

The dude. be nice. project: dudebenice.com/pages/dbnproject
Make A Difference Day: makeadifferenceday.com
Ripple Kindness Project: ripplekindness.org
Rosa's Fresh Pizza: rosasfreshpizza.com
Spread Kindness: www.spreadkindness.org

Gina's Sketchbook

Hi! I'm Gina. Welcome to my sketchbook!

Operation Frog Effect is told in journal format by eight students, one of whom draws his entries. That is where I come in. First, I needed to come up with designs for all of the characters. It was fun to read the whole book to learn more about the kids. The final art was meant to be a little rough and sketchy, done with just line work, but I needed to make sure readers knew who was who. Here are a few of my Cecilia character sketches. After a few rounds of edits, we had our cast!

TOO CLOSE TO EMILY?

MAYBE TOO SIMILAR TO SHARON?

TA-DA!

NOT GOOD SOCCER SHOES...

NEEDS SOMETHING UNIQUE... MAYBE A NECKLACE?

MEET CECILIA!

I did a lot of the rough sketches for pages on my iPad. I prefer working at home, but I was grateful that I could work even while I was out for afternoon activities with my kids. The iPad made it easy to move panels around and play with size and composition.

My first drawings are usually really rough, but they help me figure out the layout and action. Below is an early sketch for a page, followed by the final version.

Early Sketch:

Final:

The page design and content are revised after the first sketches. The drawings are simple, but they still need to communicate the ideas as clearly as possible.

If you enjoyed learning about how I made the illustrations, perhaps you could make your own comic pages. Draw four boxes on a piece of paper and tell a simple story from your day. Happy drawing!

Discussion Questions

1. In *Operation Frog Effect,* the characters come together to stand up for what they believe in. Has there been a time when you stood up for what you believe? How did that feel? What did you learn? Has there been a time when someone stood up for you? How did that feel?

2. How do you define friendship? What are the qualities you look for in a friend? Think about which characters in this book possess those qualities. Who would you want to be friends with? Why? Which characters would you not want to be friends with? Why?

3. Lots of the friendships in *Operation Frog Effect* go through changes—Aviva, Emily, and Kayley's; Kayley and Blake's; Kai and Blake's. What are some ways to fix a friendship after there have been disagreements or hurt feelings? Is there such a thing as an "unfixable" friendship? What (if anything) could happen in a friendship to make it unfixable? How do you decide whether to put more effort into a friendship . . . or to just let it go?

4. Which *Operation Frog Effect* character are you most like? Which are you most different from?

5. Sharon speaks her mind freely but is working to hold back so that others have a chance to share. Aviva has so much to say but doesn't allow herself to speak up until the end. Who are you more like? If you wanted to stretch yourself, how would you like to go about practicing a new way of interacting?

6. Kai reads for many reasons—for enjoyment, for distraction, for inspiration, and to cope with life. Why do you read? Do you ever learn from the characters in your books?

7. Kayley attempts to justify her hurtful actions and comments. She often gives a reason to defend her behavior. What do you think about the way she acts? Has anyone ever done this to you or someone you know?

8. Think of the most honest person you know. Who is that person? Do you admire him or her? What are some creative ways you can spare people's feelings and still be honest?

9. Cecilia connects to her grandmother in many ways, even though they live far apart. Some relationships are so important that they must be maintained, no matter the distance. Who is that important to you?

10. Blake faces a struggle with academics. People face many struggles, and we can't always tell that just by looking at them. Struggles often make us stronger and help us learn how to overcome adversity. Can you think of an example of a struggle someone might face that others wouldn't know about?

11. Henry tries to be funny much of the time. Why do you think he does this? Does this way of interacting work for him? Does it ever cause problems for him? How should kids know when it's appropriate to be funny and when it's better to be serious?

12. Which character do you think showed the most personal growth? Why do you think this? What kind of growth did he or she show?

13. Ms. Graham's class researches social issues. Which social issue is most important to you? Why? What are some ways that people are trying to address it? What would you do about this social issue if you were in charge of the world?

14. The homelessness social-issue group tried to immerse themselves in a way that was unsafe. What could they have done that would have kept them safe but still helped them understand the issue of homelessness? Brainstorm safe ways to make a difference.

15. What was the point of the Whistler activity? How would you feel if your teacher did the Whistler experiment with your class? Why? Do you think this lesson is applicable in today's world?

ACKNOWLEDGMENTS

In some very special classrooms during my childhood, I believed that what I thought and felt mattered. Since I was shy, I could easily have flown under the radar. Perhaps for that reason, positive feedback and acknowledgment from a teacher were like gold. I believe that teacher-child connection can shape a child's life. My extraordinary teachers are the inspiration for *Operation Frog Effect*.

My fourth-grade teacher, Mr. Alan Nubling, transformed his classroom into a mini-world, where we tackled social issues, had our own jobs, and managed pretend money. My ballet teacher, Eva Pokorny, felt like a second mom. Mr. Nubling and Mrs. Pokorny are but two of many educators who have positively affected my life or the lives of my children. I'd like to acknowledge Mrs. Brown, Mr. Busse, Mrs. Curro, Mr. Forbes, Mrs. Forbes, Alan Greenbaum, Mr. Haug, Mrs. Hinson, Mrs. Kaio, Mr. Kane, Mrs. Keefer, Mrs. Lang, Mrs. Lashkeri, Mrs. Laurentowski, Mrs. Lerned, Mrs. Liddell, John Wey Ling, Mrs. Lorimer, Mr. Lowe, Mr. Luvi, Mrs. McCook, Mrs. McCrory, Mrs. Moore, Mrs. Odell, Mrs. Ortgies, Mr. Prendergast, Mrs. Raives, Mr. Roberts, Mrs. Robbins, Mrs. Sage, Mrs. Schlemmer, Ms. Scheimer, Mr. Simonson, Ms. Sorenson, Mrs. Spellman, Mrs. Vick, Mrs. Wagner, Mr. Waters, and Mrs. White.

When I first embarked on this project, I knew it was crucial to represent the diverse and wise voices I see and hear every day as a school-based counselor in California. This story is not about any of the kids I work with—all the characters are completely fictional—but I am continuously impressed and inspired by the perseverance, strength, optimism, and wisdom I see daily in students, despite sometimes challenging circumstances. Spending time with these young people gives me hope for the future.

It was important to me to get every single one of these voices right. I wanted to portray realistic characters whose lives and voices reflect the richness of their background, but who are also well-rounded humans with both strengths and weaknesses. I found myself relying heavily on the advice and guidance of many generous readers.

I'd like to say a heartfelt thank-you to the following authenticity readers who shared insights, wisdom, support, and perspective: Alexandra Alessandri, Luvi Avendano, Keisha Carroll, Tina Chow, Kristy Curro, Andrea Del Valle, Nina Faiello-Simpson, Laura Guerra, Omario Kanjini, Chin Koh, Maria Lawson, Stephanie Lyon, Sherri Merideth-Cheatham, Luma Mufleh, Polo Orozco, Martha Zavala Perez, and Helen Wong. I am eternally grateful for the time and dedication you all put into my characters, and the feedback. If I've gotten things right, it's largely because of your thoughtful suggestions and insights; any mistakes that remain are my own. #WeNeedDiverseBooks!

Thank you to my early readers, who helped me sift through a mangled mess of unstructured ideas and turn it into something that made sense—Carie Appleton, Ben and Noah Scheerger, Chad Morris, and Deborah Halverson. A thousand thank-yous to Maya Motayne, who was an early reader at Random House. Thank you to Maria Claver and Alexandra Wilkinson for your expertise about community resources. Thank you to Shana Corey, for helping me see the forest among the trees, for discovering the frog-tastic Kermit, and for offering gentle guidance. Thank you always to Deborah Warren for your never-ending support through all the ups and downs. Thank you to art directors Maria Middleton, Bob Bianchini, and Stephanie Moss for your artistic expertise, as well as Barbara Bakowski for your keen eye for detail. Thank you to Andy Smith for the frog-errific cover. Thank you to Gina Perry for your skill in bringing Blake's story to life. Long live the frogs!

I'm sending thanks to many writers and organizations for their research on women's and social issues around the globe. Among the most helpful resources for this project were *I Am Malala* (by Malala Yousafzai and Patricia McCormick), NPR (npr.org), *USA Today* (usatoday.com), Think Progress (thinkprogress.org), Schooling for Life (schoolingforlife.net), United We Dream (unitedwedream.org), and *International Business Times* (ibtimes.co.uk).

I am also indebted to several websites for fun frog facts, including Save the Frogs! (savethefrogs.com), Smithsonian.com (smithsonianmag.com), Earth Rangers (www.earthrangers.org), and the American Museum of Natural History (amnh.org).

Thank you always to my family. To my children, for being the wonderful people you are and for helping me grow in ways you'll someday understand. Rob—I love you more every day. Thank you for your support and kindness. Mom and Dad, you've always made me feel that I mattered, that what I wanted to say mattered, and that anything was possible. Thank you for that special gift. I am eternally appreciative. The best way I can repay you is by passing it on . . . to my children, to my friends, and to my students. #KindnessMatters #PayItForward

Thank you to my Mom Tribe: Dorothy, Holly, JA, Janet, Jessica, Jill, Jodie, Joy, Kristi, Lois, Lyndall, Maria, Marjie, Michelle, Stephanie, Tara, Tina, and Valerie. I'm honored to have your company on this fantastic, trying, fulfilling journey we call parenthood.